HOOKIN' UP

What Reviewers Say About MJ Williamz's Work

Shots Fired

"MJ Williamz, in her first romantic thriller has done an impressive job of building up the tension and suspense. Williamz has a firm grasp of keeping the reader guessing and quickly turning the pages to get to the bottom of the mystery. *Shots Fired* clearly shows the author's ability to spin an engaging tale and is sure to be just the beginning of great things to follow as the author matures."
—*Lambda Literary*

"Williamz tells her story in the voices of Kyla, Echo, and Detective Pat Silverton. She does a great job with the twists and turns of the story, along with the secondary plot. The police procedure is first rate, as are the scenes between Kyla and Echo, as they try to keep their relationship alive through the stress and mistrust."—*Just About Write*

Forbidden Passions

"*Forbidden Passions* is 192 pages of bodice ripping antebellum erotica not so gently wrapped in the moistest, muskiest pantalets of lesbian horn dog high jinks ever written. While the book is joyfully and unabashedly smut, the love story is well written and the characters are multi-dimensional. ...*Forbidden Passions* is the very model of modern major erotica, but hidden within the sweet swells and trembling clefts of that erotica is a beautiful May-September romance between two wonderful and memorable characters."—*The Rainbow Reader*

Visit us at www.boldstrokesbooks.com

By the Author

Shots Fired

Forbidden Passions

Initiation by Desire

Speakeasy

Escapades

Sheltered Love

Summer Passion

Heartscapes

Love on Liberty

Love Down Under

Complications

Lessons In Desire

Hookin' Up

Hookin' Up

by

MJ Williamz

2017

HOOKIN' UP

ISBN 13: 978-1-63555-051-1

This Trade Paperback Original Is Published By
Bold Strokes Books, Inc.
P.O. Box 249
Valley Falls, NY 12185

First Edition: December 2017

Credits

Editor: Cindy Cresap
Production Design: Susan Ramundo
Cover Design By Sheri (graphicartist2020@hotmail.com)

Acknowledgments

First of all, a huge thank you to my wife, Laydin, who keeps me focused and offers her constant love and support. Next, thank you to Sarah, Inger, and Karen, for reading this book for me before I submitted it. As always, your input is invaluable to me.

I want to thank Sandy, Cindy, Rad, and all the family at Bold Strokes Books for believing in me and giving me a place for my books to call home. A special thank you to Sandy for an excellent idea for a book!

Last, but certainly not least, thank you to you, the readers, without whom none of this would be possible.

Dedication

For Laydin—For her undying love and support

Chapter One

So, I've come up with an excellent idea to help me with my problem." Leah Davis hung her purse over the back of her office chair. Dillon Franklin, her business partner and best friend, looked up from the laptop she'd been working on.

"And just what problem might that be?" she said.

"You know. When Sueann dumped me, she said I was no good in bed."

Dillon groaned internally. She remembered the day Leah had come in to tell her her partner of five years had broken up with her. Dillon wished she could offer her services to Leah. She'd been in love with her since they'd first met six years ago. But she couldn't say anything for fear she'd lose her friendship with Leah, and that would be too painful for her to take. Besides, they owned The Rainbow Kitty, the only lesbian bar in town, together. Imagine what would happen if Leah freaked out on Dillon and the mess they'd be in. So Dillon kept her feelings to herself. She played it cool.

"And just what is your excellent idea?"

"Well, you know how I was a virgin when Sueann and I got together?"

Dillon nodded.

"And I thought she would teach me all I needed to know about pleasing her?"

The subject was making Dillon decidedly uncomfortable, but she nodded again.

"So I've decided to get some experience. You know, learn how to be a better lover. Then maybe Sueann will take me back."

"Kiddo," Dillon said. "Do you really want her back? She hurt you pretty badly. Or don't you remember that part?"

"Oh, no. I do. But I think if I could please her in bed, she'd want me again."

Dillon shook her head. She was sure there was more to the breakup than just bad sex. There had to be, right? One didn't just dump someone because they weren't good in bed, did they? One might use that as an excuse, but there had to be more. Because someone could take the time to teach someone else how to be a decent lover if one really wanted.

"I still can't believe you'd take her back. I'd tell that selfish bitch exactly where to go if I ever saw her again."

"Oh, Dillon. I love how protective you are of me. But it's all good. And wait until you hear what my idea is."

"I'm all ears."

"Have you ever heard of the app Girl World?"

"No. What is it?"

"It's an app where you post a picture and a profile and then you meet women."

Dillon was immediately filled with dread. What if Leah met some nut job on this app? Was it a safe app? She felt out of control, unable to protect Leah. She didn't like the feeling, not one little bit.

"And I'm guessing you set up a profile?"

"I did." Leah beamed.

"What exactly does your profile say?"

"The truth. That I'm inexperienced in bed and want to learn to please a woman."

"You can't put that on your profile!"

"Why not? It's the truth."

"You're going to attract all kinds of weirdos. Can't you just ask people to meet you for a cup of coffee and see what happens?

See if there's chemistry? You know. Do something a little less radical?"

"Because I know how to drink coffee. I don't know how to be good at sex. That's what I need. That's what I'm looking for. Women to teach me."

"I think you're asking for trouble," Dillon said.

"And I think you're going to be surprised."

Dillon once again fought the urge to offer to teach Leah. Nothing would please her more than taking Leah to bed and teaching her all the ins and outs of loving a woman. She'd be patient and kind because she loved Leah. She'd loved her since the moment she'd first laid eyes on her. She loved the way her blond hair framed her face and made her look like an angel. She loved her blue eyes and wonderful smile that lit up a room. And she loved the dimples that bordered that smile. She loved everything about her. She let out a heavy sigh.

"There's nothing I can say to change your mind?"

"Not a thing," Leah said. "But don't worry. You'll get to check out every woman I meet."

"How's that?"

"I'm meeting them all here. You know, so you can check them out and make sure they don't seem creepy or anything."

Great, just what Dillon needed. On one hand, she didn't want to see the women who would be taking Leah home to please them. On the other, she didn't want anything bad to happen to her and appreciated the concept of vetting the women first.

"So, have you heard back from any women?"

"Sure. Lots. I'm meeting Denise, my first date, tomorrow night here."

"I'm not usually here on Saturdays."

"But I figured you'd make an exception for me."

"You know I will. So, what does this Denise look like?"

Leah grabbed her phone from her purse and opened the app. She flipped to Denise's profile and showed it to Dillon. Dillon stared hard at the picture, trying to hate the woman, but couldn't.

She looked like just any other woman on the planet. She had salt-and-pepper hair and kind looking brown eyes.

"She looks kind of old," she said.

"Yep. I figure that way she's experienced and will have lots to teach me."

"Leah, you may end up getting really hurt doing this."

"Oh, come on. Lighten up. It's something I need to do. I thought you'd support me."

Dillon sighed again.

"I'll try."

The next evening, Leah showered slowly in preparation for her big night. She washed every inch carefully, knowing she would be intimate with Denise in just a few hours. She dried off and put on a blue satin bra before she slipped a cornflower blue sundress over her head. She opened her underwear drawer and searched for something suitable. She decided to be daring and go without. She knew, after all, she was going to get laid. Or rather, she would be doing the laying. At any rate, she didn't need to waste her time with underwear. It would only be coming off.

She smoothed out her dress and checked herself out in the mirror. She thought she looked good. Good enough to sleep with anyway. She didn't feel like she was going to scare anybody off, at any rate. She laughed at the thought, but the laughter was nervous. She was terrified. She would be hooking up with a total stranger. Would they come back to her place? Or go to Denise's? She supposed that should be up to her. She decided she'd bring Denise back to her place. She'd feel safer that way.

Finally, she'd wasted enough time and it was time to go to The Kitty. She arrived and saw Dillon sitting at the bar. She quickly cut through the crowd to get to her.

"Are you really going through with this?" Dillon said.

"I am. Have you seen her?"

"Yeah. I think so. She's over in that corner."

She inclined her head to the right, but didn't turn around.

Leah turned and leaned on the bar so she could survey the room. She saw a woman who looked like Denise's photo coming toward her.

"Leah?" The woman's voice was sultry, and Leah felt a warmth flow over her.

"Yes. Denise?"

Denise smiled. It was warm and reassuring, and Leah felt certain she was going to be okay. She was doing the right thing. And Denise would be the perfect first attempt for her.

"Can I buy you a drink?" Denise said.

"Sure. I'll have a dirty martini. Oh. And, Denise? This is my friend Dillon."

"How do you do?" Dillon said as she gave Denise the once-over.

"Protective much?" Denise said.

"Very."

"Well, you don't have to worry. Leah's in good hands."

"Okay, you two," Leah said. "Settle down. Let's all have a drink and then Denise and I can take off."

"No wasting any time, huh?" Denise said.

"Why bother?"

"Good point."

"Actually, I just finished my beer, so I'm going to take off now. You two have fun." Dillon looked pointedly at Leah. "Just be careful."

Denise took the bar stool Dillon had vacated.

"So, tell me about yourself. I mean, I know what it says on your profile, which is why I'm here. But tell me something else."

"Well, let's see. I'm the co-owner of this bar. Dillon is my business partner. That takes up most of my time. What about you? What do you do?"

"I am a mechanic."

"So you're good with your hands?" Leah blushed even as she said it.

"Yes, I am. And you're cute when you blush. But my skills are not in question. Yours are. And we'll work on them until you get it right." Leah blushed again and turned away. "No. Don't turn away. I meant it. You're cute when you blush."

"Thanks. I guess."

"You don't take compliments very well, do you?"

"I don't know."

"Did your ex ever compliment you?"

Leah thought long and hard before answering.

"I don't know. I guess not. At least not often."

"Then you have lots to learn," Denise said. "More than just the obvious."

"And you'll help teach me?"

"You have me for one night. We'll work on whatever we can in that time."

They finished their drinks and butterflies appeared in Leah's stomach. She was surprised at how nervous she suddenly was. Was she doing the right thing? She took a deep breath. Yes. This is what she needed.

"Shall we get out of here?" Denise said. Leah nodded. "Your place or mine?"

"Mine, please," Leah said. "I think I'd be more comfortable there."

"Sounds good to me. I'll follow you."

Leah kept alternating her gaze between the road and Denise behind her. She was driving slowly, determined not to lose her. She wanted to be sure Denise would be with her when she got home.

She pulled into her driveway and Denise parked at the curb. Leah got out of her car and walked over to greet Denise.

"So, this is it," she said.

"Looks nice. You must do well at the bar."

"I do okay."

"Good. Shall we go inside now?"

"Yeah. I suppose we should."

Leah opened the door and let Denise in first. She closed the door behind her.

"Would you like something to drink?"

"I think I'm okay. Unless you're nervous?"

"I am. A little. But I think I'll be okay."

"Okay. So, let's sit on the couch for a minute."

Leah swallowed hard and led Denise to the living room. They sat next to each other and Denise draped an arm over Leah's shoulder. She pulled her close and kissed her forehead.

"You know, sooner or later we're going to have to go to bed. We only have one night, and apparently I have much to teach you."

"We can go now," Leah said.

"Are you sure you're ready?"

Leah was anything but ready. She nodded.

"Ready as I'll ever be."

"Good." Denise stood and took Leah's hand. She pulled her to her and kissed her lightly on the lips. The kiss sent shockwaves through Leah's body. That certainly helped her get ready.

"That was nice," she said.

"How are you at kissing? Is that a problem? Because that's hard to teach."

"I think I do okay with it."

"Good."

She kissed her again and ran her tongue along Leah's lips. Leah parted them and welcomed Denise in. She allowed her tongue to wander into Denise's mouth as well. Their tongues danced briefly before Denise pulled away.

"What?" Leah said.

"You kind of use too much tongue. Save some of that for later." She winked.

Leah was embarrassed. She couldn't even kiss. How was she supposed to be good at sex if she couldn't even get the easy stuff down?

"How much is too much?"

"You want to trace your lover's tongue, not stick yours down her throat. Hold off. Don't put as much of your tongue in my mouth. Like I said, there'll be plenty of time for you to use that tongue later. Now, let's try again."

Denise kissed Leah again. Leah opened her mouth and was conscious not to put too much of her tongue in Denise's mouth. She just ran the tip of her tongue over Denise's. But soon she was too excited and she slipped more in. She was still aware of how much she allowed in. Denise broke the kiss.

"That was much better," she said. She was breathing heavily, which Leah took as a good sign. "Now, come on. I need you. And now."

Leah was wet with her own desire and was happy she was having that effect on Denise. Denise took her hand.

"Take me to your bedroom."

Leah walked her down the hall to her Western style bedroom with a giant four-poster bed in the center. She had a solid, wooden dresser and dressing table along the sides of the room, but all she cared about at that moment was the bed, and she was pretty sure that was all Denise would notice.

Denise took Leah's dress over her head and gasped at her lack of underwear.

"I want to take you right now," she murmured against Leah's neck. "I want you so bad, but this is all about you. I need to remember that."

She reached around and unhooked Leah's bra and tossed it to the floor on top of her dress. She ran her hands down Leah's back until she got to her ass. She pressed her pelvis into Leah's.

"Fuck it," she said. "I have to have you. We can teach you after."

"But..."

"No. No buts. I'm sorry, Leah, but you're too hot. I want to fuck you and I have to do it. There will be plenty of time for you to please me when I'm through."

Leah wasn't sure what to think. She wanted Denise, too. She craved her touch, needed her inside her.

"Fine. Take me. I need you, too. But then promise me you'll teach me."

"I will. I'll be hot and ready for you then, too. You should have no trouble getting me off. Especially under my guidance."

She slid her fingers into Leah's wet curls.

"You really do want me, don't you?" Denise said.

"Yes. Please. Can we lie down?"

"Sure. You lie down and I'll strip and then join you."

Leah did as she was instructed. She lay on the bed and watched as Denise removed her clothes. Her body was amazing. Not too tight, but not too soft either.

"I love your body," she said.

"Thanks. I love yours."

Denise climbed up onto the bed with Leah and immediately started pleasing her. She sucked first one nipple then the other while her fingers found her wet center.

Leah let out a low moan. She couldn't believe how good Denise was making her feel. She wanted to learn to make women feel like that. The thought lasted only a moment before she closed her eyes and lost herself in the sensations. It took no time for Denise to bring her to one powerful orgasm then another. She felt her whole world explode into tiny pieces. She finally got herself together and opened her eyes to see Denise staring into them.

"You liked that, huh?" Denise smiled.

"Yeah, I did."

"Okay. Now you get to do that to me."

Leah was nervous again, even as she continued to twitch and throb in the aftermath of her climaxes. Her stomach was in knots. It was time to show another person, not just Sueann, how lousy she was in bed. She'd never been more terrified.

"Calm down, Leah. Your heart's racing." Denise had her head resting on Leah's chest. "I mean, not like it did when you came. I mean like you're scared to death."

"I am scared. What if I'm as bad as my ex said I was? What then?"

"I'm not expecting perfection. I came here tonight knowing you were inexperienced. I'm only here to help, okay?"

Leah nodded.

"Okay. Can we kiss again?"

"Sure."

Denise moved up her body until their lips met. Leah was careful not to use too much tongue, but to enjoy the feelings Denise was creating with hers. Soon, she was all worked up again and ready to give it her best shot.

She kissed down Denise's chest until she got to a nipple. She sucked it hard into her mouth.

"Okay. Lesson one," Denise said. "Nipples are sensitive. Don't suck it like you're a vacuum cleaner. Suck it tenderly, lovingly. Otherwise it hurts. Which might work for some women, but it doesn't work for most."

"Got it. How about I forget your nipples and just get to the good stuff?"

"That's not a good idea, either. Nipples are fun. When loved correctly, they can increase the pleasure for your partner, which will get her even wetter and more ready for you."

Leah sighed deeply.

"Okay. I'll try again."

She lowered her head and licked Denise's hard nipple. She ran her tongue over and around it before gently taking it into her mouth. When it was in her mouth, she ran her tongue over it some more. Denise didn't say anything, so Leah thought she must be on the right track.

"Oh yeah. That's good," Denise finally said.

She kept at it, and Denise gently tapped her on her head.

"Okay, Leah. I need you now. Please me, baby. Take me where I took you."

Leah was excited then. One thing she loved was the taste of a woman. She didn't understand what she'd been doing wrong, but she was happy to go down on Denise for instructions.

She spread Denise's legs and climbed between them. She gazed hungrily at the sight before her. Denise was pink and swollen and wet and looked delicious. She lowered her head and began to lick and suck on everything she found. Denise was delicious, just as she'd known she would be.

"Whoa there, cowgirl," Denise said. "There's no method to your madness there. You're going all over the place. You want to know what someone once told me about eating pussy? Use your tongue and write the alphabet in cursive. Why don't you try that?"

"Is that what you do?"

"No. But I know what I'm doing at this point. Every woman is going to be different, so even if you get me to come, it doesn't mean what you do to me will work on the next woman you're with. I think it's a good place for you to start."

Leah took a deep breath and began again. She made an A, took a breath and made a B.

"Don't pause. Just do it in one motion. A, then B, then C."

"Upper or lower case?"

"Lower."

"Okay."

Leah began again. This seemed easy enough. She got through the alphabet and Denise put her hand on her head.

"That's great. That's a good start. I'm feeling it now. Now dip your tongue inside. Lick all around."

Leah did as she'd been told. She buried her tongue deep inside Denise and licked up all the juices that were flowing there. She was in heaven and Denise was writhing on the bed.

"Now suck my clit, baby. Gentle. And lick it while you do."

Leah ran her tongue along the length of her until she arrived at her nerve center. She could feel it throbbing between her lips. She sucked lightly and flicked at it with her tongue.

"Holy Jesus. I think you've got it. Don't stop."

Leah smiled to herself. She had no intention of stopping. Encouraged, she sucked harder and licked faster. She was determined to make Denise come.

"Whoa. Stop," Denise said. "Too much. Why didn't you keep doing what you were doing? You had me on the brink."

"I thought I did keep doing what you said."

"No. You started licking faster and harder. You took me right out of the space."

Leah felt dejected. She'd been so close. How could she have failed?

"I'm sorry. I thought it would make you feel better."

"Well, you didn't. You had me close though. We'll call that a win for tonight. I think you have a good head start now."

"Thanks, Denise."

"I'm going to head home now."

"Okay. Look, I really am sorry."

"It's okay. I came here knowing you were inexperienced. I only hope you remember a little of what I taught you."

"I'll try."

Leah stood at the front door looking at her feet.

"Hey, you're a beautiful woman. And you're smart. You'll get the hang of it. I've no doubt. All it's going to take is practice and patience in a partner."

Leah wanted to ask, to beg, for another chance, but knew the deal. Each of these was a one-night thing and Denise had taught her all she felt she could in their one night together.

"Take care, Leah," Denise said. She kissed her cheek and left.

Chapter Two

Dillon was prepping the bar for opening Monday morning. She kept checking her watch, wondering where Leah was. She needed her either at the bar to finish setting up, or to run to the bank with the weekend deposits. She was getting annoyed. It wasn't like Leah to be late. Suddenly, she realized she hadn't heard from Leah since her date Saturday night. She felt a pang of fear and her annoyance slipped away. She was worried about her. She knew nothing about this Denise woman. She wouldn't even know where to find her. Shit. Where was Leah?

She damned near jumped out of her skin when the bells on the front door jingled signaling someone's arrival. She turned to see Leah waltz in and head to the office. She followed close on her heels.

"Slow down there, woman," Dillon said. "I need to know how your date went. Come on out and talk to me. I want to know everything."

The latter wasn't true. Dillon really didn't want to know details about Leah's sexual encounter, but she knew she'd feel better hearing that it was really a one-time thing and she held out hope that Leah had changed her mind about using this whole app thing after all.

"There's nothing to tell."

"Nothing? Nothing happened?"

Dillon's heart soared at the thought.

"No. Things happened. Things I apparently am terrible at."

"Oh. I'm sorry, Leah." She pulled Leah into her arms and held her tight. Leah pushed her away.

"No. It's okay. I learned some valuable information. I've improved my technique already. But there's more I need to learn. So I won't be terrible."

"She didn't say you were terrible." Dillon was in disbelief.

"I turned her off. But I don't want to talk about it."

Dillon stared after Leah as she left the office. How could she possibly turn anybody off? She was the hottest woman Dillon knew. And from the way Denise had been looking at her Saturday night, she clearly felt the same. And yet Leah had turned her off? She needed more information, so she joined Leah behind the bar.

"How did you turn her off? I'm going to need some explanation."

"I told you, I don't want to talk about it."

"Please, Leah."

"No. It's not going to happen. Now, have you made the deposit from the weekend yet?"

Dillon let out a deep breath.

"Fine. Be that way. And no, I haven't made the deposit yet. You can go ahead and get it ready."

"Thanks."

Dillon finished getting the bar set up. They would open in a half hour. So she had some time to relax before she'd take her place behind the bar to greet the patrons. She walked into the office to see Leah still counting cash.

"Are you just not focused today or what?"

"No. Holy shit, Dillon. We kicked ass this weekend."

"Yeah? That's awesome."

"Yeah it is. Give me some time to get this deposit finished. Then I'll head to the bank."

"Right on."

Dillon sat in her chair across the desk from Leah and watched her add the remainder of the money. She wondered anew what had happened Saturday night, but knew she had to give her the time and space she needed to get over it. She was curious if she still planned to keep using that stupid app.

Finally, Leah put the deposit in her bag and rose.

"I'll be back."

"Okay. And maybe we can talk when you get back?"

"And maybe not."

Dillon watched her walk out the door and get in her car. Why was Leah being so secretive about Saturday night? They normally talked about everything together. She knew Leah had been a virgin when she got together with Sueann. And Leah hadn't been too ashamed to tell her Sueann had dumped her because she couldn't please her. So now, on this mission to learn to please a woman, it seemed logical that they would talk about how it was going. She shook her head. It must have been bad. Really bad. And, again, there was nothing she could do to make it better.

Leah got back to the bar just before Dillon switched on the neon lights to signify they were open for business. Leah was smiling and had a slight spring in her step.

"You seem like you're feeling better," Dillon said.

"I am. That deposit was amazing. It was our biggest one ever. I'm going to go enter it in the system before we get too busy."

"That's great. And I'm glad to see you smiling again."

"That's only partly due to the deposit." Leah called over her shoulder as she walked into the office. Dillon followed her and leaned against the doorjamb so she could see both Leah and the bar.

"And what's the other part due to?"

"A woman named Donna has agreed to meet me Saturday."

"Donna? You got something for women whose names start with D?"

Leah laughed.

"Nope. It's just the way they're playing out."

"Okay, well let me see this woman."

Leah handed her phone to her.

"She's pretty, don't you think?"

"She's older again. You like older women suddenly?"

"Look, I'd take damned near anyone who is willing to date me now. I need someone to teach me, and if she's willing to take the time, I'm all over it."

Dillon wanted to point out that her name started with a D. And that she'd be more than happy to teach her. But she kept her mouth shut. She couldn't say anything. She was past due to be with a woman. She wasn't into one-night stands, but she knew when she needed a woman's touch, and that time was drawing near. She told herself it must be all the nonsense with Leah and let the thoughts go.

"So what's the plan with this one?"

"Same as before. We'll meet here Saturday so you can check her out. Sound good?"

"Sure." Dillon tried to sound anything but depressed. "Sounds great. But I have to ask. Why strangers?"

"Who am I supposed to ask? My next-door neighbor?" Leah laughed.

Dillon bit her tongue.

"Seriously," Leah went on. "They have to be strangers, women I'm not likely to see ever again since apparently, I'm really not good at this."

How bad could she be? She was gorgeous. Surely if she just did what came naturally, she'd bring any woman to her knees. But Sueann and now this Denise had told her she was lousy. God, Dillon wished she could find out for herself.

Saturday night rolled around again, and Leah walked into the bar to find Dillon in her usual spot at the bar. She seemed to be lilting a little.

"You okay?" Leah said.

"Sure."

Leah checked out her eyes. They were glossy. Oh, my God, Dillon was drunk. That was a very uncommon experience.

"Why are you so hammered?" Leah said.

"I don't know. Just felt like it."

"Dillon, you're slurring your words. I need to get you home."

"I'm fine."

"No, you're not."

"You're right. I can't drive. I'll call a cab. Don't worry."

"Give me your car keys."

Dillon fished in her pocket for her keys. She took her car key off and handed it to Leah.

"Thanks."

"Thank you," Dillon said. "By the way, I haven't seen your stupid date yet."

"That's odd. I'm even a little late."

Dillon shrugged.

"Don't know what to tell you." She looked up at the mirror behind the bar. "Oh, wait. I think she just got here. She's dressed in all leather. Interesting. Be careful, Leah."

"Always, Dillon."

The woman in leather approached Leah and Dillon.

"I'm Donna," she said. "You must be Leah?"

"I am. And this is my best friend, Dillon."

"Nice to meet you. You guys partying or what?"

"I'm not. I just got here," Leah said. "But Dillon's had a few."

"And now it's time for me to call a cab. You two have fun tonight."

"Oh, don't you worry. We will," Donna said. She placed her arm protectively around Leah.

Leah wasn't sure about her level of comfort with Donna. She seemed nice enough, and what did it hurt if she had her arm around her? She was going home with her that night. There was no need for games.

"Can I buy you a drink?" Donna said. "Or should we just get out of here?"

"I think I'd like a dirty martini."

"Excellent. A dirty martini for my dirty minx."

Leah forced herself to laugh.

Donna signaled for the bartender and ordered their drinks. While she waited, she turned back to Leah.

"So, how bad are you in bed? I mean, really?"

Leah looked around, unable to believe Donna had asked that question in a crowded bar. But no one seemed to have noticed.

"If you don't mind," she said, "we own this place so I'd really rather not discuss that here."

Donna shrugged and handed Leah her drink.

"Suit yourself. I just wanted to know what I'm in for."

"You'll have a lot of teaching to do."

"Well, I kind of got that from your profile. It took guts, though, I've got to say, for you to post that."

"Well, it's what I need. It's the only reason I'd sign up for one of those sites."

"Some women actually use them to find potential life partners."

Leah shook her head.

"Oh, no. Once I know what I'm doing, I'm going to get with my ex, show her I know what I'm doing, and win her back."

"After she dumped you?"

"Yep. I know, it probably sounds crazy."

"More than a little. Someone dumps me and I say good riddance."

"It's not that simple with us. She never said she doesn't love me." Leah lowered her voice. "Just that I don't satisfy her."

"So you figure you learn how to satisfy a woman and she'll want you back. I see what you're saying, but it still sounds to me like you're opening yourself up to a heart break."

"You don't know Sueann."

"No. No, I don't."

They finished their drinks.

"You need another one?" Donna said.

"No, thanks. Let's get out of here."

"You've got it."

Donna took Leah's hand and led her out to the parking lot.

"Which car is yours?" she said.

"That one." Leah pointed to the green Kia Soul.

"Great. I'll follow you."

Leah watched as Donna walked over to a truck and climbed in. She waited until she was behind her before she pulled out. When she arrived at her house, she took a deep breath. Donna was different from Denise. And Sueann. And they were the only two women she'd been with. She didn't know what it was, but something about her made Leah more nervous. She shook it off. They both knew what they were there for, and Donna sure carried herself as an experienced woman. Leah was certain she would learn a lot that night.

As soon as Leah had closed the front door between them, Donna pressed her against it and kissed her hard on her mouth. Leah remembered what Denise had said about not using too much tongue. She kissed Donna back with a fervency she hadn't known she'd had.

Donna broke the kiss and backed up some.

"Do you have a short tongue or something?" she said.

"I don't think so. Why?"

"I don't know, but I think kissing should be the first thing we work on. You act like you're afraid of my tongue. Don't be. Let your tongue loose, Leah. Let it roll around with mine. Light me up with it."

Leah was confused. She had been trying to do what Denise had told her, but apparently, that wasn't working with Donna. She kissed her back and used her whole tongue. She was getting wetter by the moment and only hoped Donna was, too. She felt like she would implode from the fire burning inside when Donna finally broke the kiss.

"Come on. Let's go to bed. I need to have you," she said.

Leah led her down the hall to her bedroom. Donna wasted no time taking Leah's dress over her head. She saw her breasts overflowing from her bra and reached around to unhook it. She held Leah's breasts in her hands and ran her thumbs over her hardening nipples. She slid her hands lower and cupped Leah's bare ass. She traced her hip bones and soft upper thighs as she brought her hands around to tease her.

Leah spread her legs to welcome Donna's touch, but it didn't come. She opened her eyes to see Donna smiling at her.

"Time for me to get undressed now so you can show me what kind of skills you've got."

"But...but..."

"If you treat me right, I'll please you later. If not, you're on your own."

Leah was shaking in her need. She swallowed hard and took a deep breath to try to get control of her body. She looked down at the hard body of Donna lying spread out before her on the bed and decided she could do it. She'd learned enough from Denise that she felt she could please Donna. And then she'd get relief.

She decided to start at Donna's small, firm breasts. She licked her nipples and felt them grow. She lowered her mouth over one and sucked it softly and ran her tongue over it.

"What's the matter?" Donna said. "Are you afraid?"

"Hm?" Leah didn't let go of the nipple.

"Those things are attached. They're not coming off. Suck it like you mean it."

Leah was confused, but determined to make Donna come. She needed her in the worst way, and that wasn't going to happen unless she got her off. So she sucked her nipple deep into her mouth and played with it with her tongue.

"That's it. Now you're on the right path. Fuck, that feels good."

Leah ran her hand down Donna's tight belly and played her fingers in the wetness between her legs. She wanted to taste her. She needed to. She believed she could follow Denise's instructions and at least get her warmed up.

She released her grip on her nipple and kissed down her body until she could position herself between her legs. She lowered her head and began to write the alphabet in cursive with her tongue.

"Okay, woman. That's a start," Donna said. "Now fuck me. I mean really fuck me. Like you mean it. I'm ready for you."

Leah wasn't sure what Donna meant. She dipped her tongue inside as deep as it could go and lapped at all the juices flowing there.

"Fingers," Donna said.

Leah slipped two fingers inside Donna and moved them in and out, plunging them deeper with each thrust. Donna was arching off the bed, meeting each thrust.

"More," she said. "Give me more."

Leah wasn't sure what she meant, so she slid another finger in and continued to pump in and out. She licked her way to Donna's swollen clit and took it in her mouth. She licked it with her tongue while she sucked it between her lips.

"Oh dear God," Donna said. "I'm so close."

Leah kept up at a frantic pace until Donna tapped her on her head.

"I'm not sure what's up, but it's just not happening."

"Can I keep trying? Please?"

"I'm getting sore. So, no. You did okay. You just need to learn how to take a woman over the edge. You had me close. I don't know what to tell you. You just need to seal the deal. Good luck."

"But, Donna..." Leah looked pleadingly at Donna.

"I told you. You're on your own. I'll see you around."

Leah shut the door and fought tears. She had come so close to giving Donna an orgasm. But she hadn't. She felt dejected, but even feeling that way, she was still aroused beyond words. She padded to her bedroom and climbed up into the big bed. She piled her pillows behind her head and ran her hands up and down the length of her body. It tingled everywhere she touched. She pinched her nipples and twisted them. She kept opening and closing her legs as more and more fluids flowed the more she tweaked her nipples.

She slid one hand down her stomach to the wetness between her legs. She slipped her fingers inside and stroked her tender walls before her clit begged for attention. She gave it the attention it needed by rubbing frantically on it until her whole body tensed up, she felt white heat explode through her body, and then she relaxed onto the bed.

Although she was satiated, she still hadn't learned how to please anybody but herself, and that wasn't going to get Sueann back.

She closed her eyes and cried herself to sleep.

CHAPTER THREE

Dillon woke up the next morning with a throbbing head and a dry mouth.

"Ooh," she groaned. "Too much tequila and beer last night."

She got out of bed slowly and made her way to her entry hall. She peeked out at her driveway. No truck. Great. So she hadn't driven home. That's right. Leah had taken her keys. Leah. It was all her fault anyway. If she hadn't started this stupid sex search she was on, Dillon wouldn't be drinking like a fish to drown her sorrows.

Dillon started a pot of coffee and took two ibuprofen with a glass of water. That should help the head. She sat at her kitchen table to wait for the coffee when her phone rang. She reached into her pajama pockets. No phone. It was ringing incessantly. She hurried, as fast as she could go, to her bedroom, but the ringing stopped before she got there. She sat on the bed while the dizziness cleared and checked her phone. A missed call from Leah and a voice mail. She listened to the voice mail.

"Hey, Dillon, it's me. I've got your keys. I thought maybe I'd give them to you over breakfast? What do you say? I know I could use some grease this morning. Call me back."

Dillon didn't even stop to think. She called her back.

"Hey, Dillon. How are you today?"

"Horrible. And you?"

"About the same."

"Oh, no. What happened?" Dillon didn't like to think of Leah feeling horrible, but if she'd crashed and burned again, maybe this nonsense would end.

"We can talk about it over breakfast. Or lunch for me, rather. I want a chili burger with extra onions."

Dillon laughed.

"Okay. Give me fifteen minutes to get ready and then swing on by. I'll leave the door unlocked."

"Sounds good. See you then."

Dillon climbed into the shower and let the hot water wash away the disgusted feeling that covered her. She felt clean and human when she stepped out of the shower a few minutes later. She must have taken a longer shower than she thought because when she walked out to the kitchen to get a cup of coffee, with only her towel wrapped around her waist, she was shocked to see Leah at the kitchen table.

"What the—?"

"I'm sorry," Leah said. "I got here a little early."

Dillon beat a hasty retreat to her room where she quickly dressed in shorts and a T-shirt. She walked back out to the kitchen.

"Sorry about that," she said.

"No, I'm sorry. I shouldn't have gotten here so early. For heaven's sake, you're allowed to wander around your house half naked if you want."

"Thank you for your permission." She crossed the room and kissed Leah on the top of her head. "How's the coffee?"

"Delicious. Nice and strong."

"Oh, good. Just what I need. Do we have time for me to have a cup before we go?"

"Sure. Relax and enjoy it. I'm not in any hurry."

"Me neither, really. Except I've got a wicked case of the munchies."

"Okay. We'll get you all greased up. But relax and enjoy your coffee for now."

"So, you want to tell me about your night last night?" It was actually the last thing Dillon wanted to hear about, but she figured she'd rather be a sounding board so she had some idea of what was going on rather than be totally in the dark.

"It was horrible. Just horrible. Can't we go to the restaurant to talk about this?"

"Sure. I thought this might be a little more private, but if you want to talk in public, that's fine by me."

"No. You're right. Of course. It's just that I'm starving and I'm still not sure yet how much to tell you."

"Leah, I've been your best friend for six years. Is there anything you can't tell me?"

Leah grew even more sullen.

"I don't know. I just don't know. Plus, I'm so confused."

"How so?"

"Finish your coffee. I'm starving."

They drove to their favorite restaurant and placed their orders. Dillon leaned back against her booth and surveyed the mostly empty restaurant. Their conversation should be private enough.

"So, what's the deal?" she said.

"Women. I don't understand them."

"Why do you think I'm still single? I'd rather be married to the bar than deal with a woman."

"Don't you miss the companionship, though?"

"Sometimes. But I keep myself busy enough," Dillon said.

"Don't you miss the sex?"

Dillon laughed.

"Sure I do. Now what happened last night?"

"Well, here's the deal. Everything Denise told me to do, everything she corrected me on, Donna contradicted."

Dillon tried to hide her smirk behind her hand.

"You think it's funny."

"No. No, I don't. But, kiddo, every woman is different. Just because one woman wants it a certain way doesn't mean they're all going to want it that way. You need to learn to tell what each woman wants."

"And how do I tell?"

They were silent while the waitress deposited their food.

"You pay attention to the way they move, the sounds they make, the things they say."

Leah just shook her head.

"The thing is, these women are supposed to be helping me. If one says one thing and the other says the exact opposite, like *exact* opposite, how am I supposed to ever learn?"

"So you agree this isn't the way to go about doing this?" Dillon was hopeful.

"Oh, no. Au contraire. I'm more determined than ever. I'm going to get the opinions of as many women as I can and go with the majority rules approach."

"So just exactly how many women do you plan to sleep with?"

"As many as I can."

Dillon's appetite suddenly diminished. She pushed her plate away.

"I thought you were hungry," Leah said.

"Yeah, not so much anymore."

"Why not?"

"Leah, I'm worried about you. I don't know that sleeping with every woman in town is the healthiest way to cope with the loss of Sueann."

"I'm not coping, Dillon. I'm learning. And once I'm good in bed, I'll get Sueann back again."

"Are you serious? Leah, please don't get your hopes up. Sueann may have moved on by then."

"I doubt it. I was the love of her life for five years. It's going to take longer than a few months to get over me."

"Women can be fickle. That's all I'm saying."

Dillon had never liked Sueann. Sure, she'd been jealous as hell of her relationship with Leah, but there was more to it. Something about her struck Dillon as slimy, not trustworthy. She wouldn't have been surprised if Sueann wasn't seeing someone else when she split up with Leah. But she kept her mouth shut. Clearly, Leah would defend her to the ends of the earth.

"And what makes you such an expert? When was the last time you even had a date?"

"What does that matter? This is about you, not me," Dillon said.

"I'm just pointing out that you got dumped. Hard. And you haven't even gotten back in the saddle and it's been how long now?"

"Ten years, but who's counting?"

"Well, my hoochie can't wait ten years. I need to learn how to treat another woman so I can show off to Sueann and get her back."

Dillon had to laugh at Leah's vernacular.

"What?"

Dillon just shook her head.

"Nothing. You're exasperating me, but you're also cracking me up."

"Why?"

But Leah had started laughing, too. She seemed to have realized that the terminology she had used was rather amusing.

Dillon moved her plate closer and began to eat again. She was hungover as hell, and the food was just what she needed to soak up the alcohol in her system.

"So who's the lucky woman this weekend?" she said.

"I don't know. I haven't heard from anyone yet."

Leah watched Dillon eat what was left of her breakfast. She admired her. She always had. She was a very handsome woman and quite unlike Leah in every way. She had dark skin and eyes and was several inches taller than she was. She knew Franklin wasn't her birth last name, but Dillon had never told her why. And Leah didn't pry. While she was pretty much an open book, Dillon kept things to herself. She was a very private person. Just once, Leah wished she'd open up to her, but she knew that wasn't going to happen. And she had too much respect for her to pry.

"Really?" Dillon said. "I thought they'd be beating down your door."

Leah laughed.

"I wish. No. So far, Donna and Denise have been the only two to actually reply."

"Maybe people don't believe your profile is real. I mean, a beautiful woman asking for help with her sex techniques? That's like a dream come true. They probably think you're a fake."

"Oh, I hope not. This is serious, as you know."

"Yeah. I know. But do they?"

"What can I do?" Leah said.

"I don't know," Dillon said. "I don't know anything about those apps."

Leah got up out of her side of the booth and sat next to Dillon.

"Here." She handed the phone to Dillon. "What else should I say?"

Dillon pushed the phone back without looking at it.

"Look. I really don't know."

"You didn't even look at it."

"What can I say? I don't need to know what you're doing in your free time."

"How can you say that?" Leah said. "You're my best friend. I trust you to help keep me safe. I need your help here. Please?"

Dillon stared hard at Leah until Leah started to squirm.

"Fine," she said. "Here. Give me your phone."

"Is the picture okay? Should I put something more provocative on there?"

"No," Dillon said quickly. "The picture is fine. You look great. It shows your personality with that smile. Keep the picture. Now where's the profile?"

Leah scrolled down on the page. Dillon read out loud.

"Single white woman needs to learn to please a woman sexually. I'm clean and you should be, too. Hit me up if you're willing to take a night to teach me how to make a woman feel good."

"What should I change?" Leah said.

"Nothing." Dillon shoved the phone back at her. "Not a thing."

"What's wrong? You seem pissed."

"You know I don't like this business. I can't believe you made me read your profile. You're basically opening yourself up to strangers. I don't like it, Leah. Not one bit."

"But I need your help. I need to make this happen."

"Okay. Fine. For what you're using it for, I think your profile is fine."

"Then why haven't more women contacted me?"

As if on cue, her phone buzzed.

"Is that a potential instructor?" Dillon said.

"It is indeed." Leah was all smiles as she opened the app.

"What's she say?"

"Her name is Chris. She's soft butch and thinks she can help me. She wants to meet me."

"Well, there you go then. Someone new."

"I know. And look. She's cute."

She showed Dillon the phone.

"She's not my type," Dillon said.

Leah rolled her eyes.

"I don't know why you're being so difficult about this. I need to learn and these women are willing to help. I'd think you'd be happy for me."

"Whatever. Where is our waitress? I want to pay our bill and get out of here."

"I'll pay my share."

"Don't be ridiculous. You got me out of the house and made me eat. For that, I am eternally grateful and don't mind buying you a chili burger."

Leah's phone buzzed again.

"She wants to meet tonight. Do you mind if I'm a little late tomorrow? And would you mind hanging at the bar tonight?"

"After last night, the last place I want to be is back at the bar tonight," Dillon said.

"Please? I really want to meet her. I'm thinking she could be the one who really teaches me something that makes sense."

"Okay. Fine. I'll hang out tonight. But how late do you think you'll be tomorrow? It'll be Monday after all. And there will be lots to do."

"I'll try to be on time. I promise. I might just be a half hour late or so."

Dillon let out a heavy sigh.

"That's fine. I mean, it'll have to be."

Leah leaned over and kissed Dillon on the cheek as she frantically typed her response to Chris.

After breakfast, Leah went dress shopping and bought a new blue dress and blue pumps. She was going to look amazing for Chris, since she believed Chris was the one. She couldn't put her finger on it, but there was just something in her eyes, her smile, that made Leah believe she had the confidence and patience to teach her all she needed to know.

She went home and soaked in a long, hot bath full of lavender oils. After, she showered and dried off, carefully patting every spot she knew Chris would touch just minutes later. When she was clean and dry, she put on her blue bra and slipped her dress on. She guided her feet into her shoes and looked in the mirror. She looked good. Damned good, even if she did say so herself.

Leah grabbed her keys and drove to The Kitty. She parked next to Dillon's truck and said a silent prayer that Dillon wouldn't be in the same shape she'd been in the night before. She entered the bar and found Dillon at the bar drinking cola.

"No beers for you?" Leah said.

"Hell, no." Dillon laughed. "No beer and no tequila for me for a long time."

Leah laughed, too.

"That's probably not a bad thing. So, have you spotted Chris yet?"

"I'm not sure, but I think she's sitting in the corner by the jukebox."

Leah carefully scanned the room and tried to look as casual as possible, though her heart was thumping in her chest. She saw a woman who did indeed look like Chris. She was looking into her beer.

"So what do I do now?" Leah said. "Do I wait for her to come up to me? Or do I approach her?"

"How should I know? This is your gig."

"There's that support I count on."

"Sorry. But I seriously don't know. You could approach her, but then I wouldn't get to meet her. And isn't that the whole point of me being here?"

"I suppose you're right. I could go talk to her and bring her up to the bar."

"You could do that."

Leah hadn't been watching the mirror and almost jumped out of her skin when she heard a soft, melodic voice say her name. She turned to see Chris, a woman of moderate height with short dark hair much like Dillon's, standing there. She had bright green eyes and an easy smile.

"Hi. You must be Chris."

"I am. I hope I'm not interrupting anything?" She looked from Leah to Dillon and back again.

"No. Chris, this is Dillon. She's my best friend."

"Ah. So she's here to make sure I'm not some wacko, huh?"

Leah laughed at her brazenness.

"Pretty much."

"Well," Chris said. "What's the verdict?"

"I don't know yet," Dillon said. Leah cringed. "Pull up a seat and join us."

"Gladly."

Chris sat on the bar stool on the other side of Leah.

"Can I buy you a beer?" she said.

"I'd like a dirty martini," Leah said. "Dillon?"

"I'll have a beer."

Leah shot her a surprised look, but didn't say anything. Dillon seemed serious about checking out Chris and Leah wasn't going to complain.

"So, what are your intentions?" Dillon said.

Leah laughed nervously.

"Well, I read Leah's profile and was hoping to do what she asked. That is, teach her to make love to a woman."

Dillon didn't say a word, and Leah was surprised at how easily Chris had said that. She didn't seem embarrassed in the least. She liked her easy confidence. She liked Chris. She was now sure she'd been right. Chris would be the one to really teach her what she needed to know.

"Well then," Dillon finally said. "I guess my work here is done. Thanks for the beer. You two enjoy yourselves."

And with that, she left the bar.

"She barely touched her beer," Chris said.

"She's a bit hungover."

"Ah. Well, nice of her to let me buy her a beer anyway. She must really care about you."

"Yep. We've been best friends for six years now. I'd do anything for her and she'd do anything for me."

"Yeah? Well then, why isn't she teaching you the finer points of sex?"

Leah felt a warm sensation flow over her. *What was that?*

"That would be weird. We're friends, not lovers."

"Got it."

"So you about ready to get out of here?" Leah said.

"Lead the way."

CHAPTER FOUR

Her nerves were back in a big way once she was inside her house. Chris seemed okay with letting her take the lead, and that wasn't her style. Chris just stood there taking in her house.

"Nice place you've got here," she said.

"Thanks. It's not much, but it's mine."

"Nonsense. It's nice. You must do okay for yourself."

"Dillon and I own The Rainbow Kitty, so yeah, I guess we do okay."

"Nice."

"Would you like another beer?"

"No. I'm fine. So how do you want to do this?"

"What do you mean?"

"Well," Chris said. "I've never actually taught a woman how to make love before. So, what shall we do? Just head to the bedroom and go for it?"

"I guess. I don't know."

"Are you nervous?"

"A little. Yeah."

"Okay, well, we can just sit down and talk for a while."

"That would be nice. Thanks."

They sat on the couch, almost close enough to touch, but not quite.

"Tell me about yourself, Chris. What do you do for a living?" Chris sat with her hands folded between her legs.

"I'm a web designer. It's a fun job and pays well, so I can't complain."

"Very cool."

Leah looked at Chris, and her stomach did a flip. She was quite possibly the most handsome woman she'd ever seen. Outside of Dillon anyway. She loved the way the lights caused her green eyes to glisten. She wanted her in a big way. She wanted to be taken by her, but was terrified about actually trying to please her.

"What are you thinking about?" Chris said.

"Just how good looking you are." She paused. "And how desperately I want you. And how terrified I am about trying to please you."

"So, what are the rules? Do I get to take you, too? Or do I just have to teach you how to take me?"

"Oh no. You get to take me. Please. I need you to take me."

"I thought you'd never ask."

She closed the distance between them and gently brushed her lips over Leah's. Leah felt her nipples harden. Her response to Chris was visceral, carnal even. She needed her, and sooner rather than later.

Chris gently probed Leah's lips with her tongue, and Leah opened her mouth and welcomed her in. She was suddenly apprehensive. She didn't know how to kiss. She pulled away.

"What's up?" Chris said.

"I should warn you. I don't know how to kiss either."

"Kissing is natural. Just do what feels right."

"But apparently, sometimes I use too much tongue and sometimes I don't use enough."

"Seriously. I'm in a bad place here. I want you so bad I might explode just sitting here, so please. Just relax and go with it. Follow my lead."

She kissed Leah again, and this time Leah allowed her own tongue to wander into Chris's mouth. She was warm and moist and tasted slightly of beer. Leah wanted to taste the rest of her. She wanted her tongue in other warm and moist spots on her body. But before she'd be able to concentrate, she needed this yearning to be quenched.

Chris leaned over her on the couch, and soon Leah was lying on her back, her dress hiked up and her legs wrapped around Chris's middle. Chris ground into her, and Leah wanted to beg her to take her right then. Chris finally sat up, breathing heavily.

"Let's take this to the bedroom. You're too fine to have me fucking you on a couch."

It took a moment for the fog of desire to lift from Leah's head, but soon it did and she sat up and smoothed her dress.

"Of course." Her voice shook. "This way."

She led Chris back to her bedroom and they began kissing again. This time, Chris unzipped her dress and let it fall to the floor. She ran her hand down to between Leah's legs, and Leah knew she was hot and wet. She was glad she didn't have on panties, as she was sure they would have been embarrassingly soaked.

"You're so wet," Chris murmured against her lips. "And hot. I've got to have you now."

She unhooked Leah's bra and tossed it on the floor. She bent to take first one nipple then the other into her mouth. She sucked and licked and teased them to attention. Leah dug her fingernails into her back.

"Oh, dear God," she said.

"Here. Sit on the edge of your bed," Chris said.

Leah didn't hesitate. She sat down and spread her legs. Chris knelt between them and placed her knees over her shoulders. She buried her face between her legs, and Leah squealed when she felt her tongue lick her between her lips. Chris sucked her lips as she licked them and Leah gripped the bedspread hard.

Chris ran her tongue lower and dipped in deep inside. Leah was moving around, grinding her pussy into Chris's face. Chris stayed with her. She replaced her tongue with her fingers and placed her lips around Leah's hard clit. She sucked and licked as she fucked her with her fingers, and soon Leah was crying out, her whole body convulsing as the orgasms washed over her.

But Chris wasn't done. She continued thrusting her fingers. She found Leah's special spot inside and rubbed it while she continued to suckle her clit. Leah pressed her face into her as she shuddered again and again as she climaxed several more times. Spent, she lay back on the bed.

Leah heard, rather than saw, Chris unbuckle her belt and let her jeans slip to the floor. It brought her out of her stupor. She sat up to watch Chris take off the remainder of her clothes, revealing a firm body just as she'd expected.

"Move over," Chris said. "I'm coming up."

Leah moved over and made room for Chris to lie next to her. Her gaze ran all over Chris's body. She couldn't wait to have a go at it. And then the nerves were back. This was her chance. But could she do it?

"You ready to return the favor?" Chris said.

"I think so. God, I want to."

"So where do you have a problem?" Chris said gently.

"Pretty much sealing the deal. I've learned to make women feel good, just not good enough."

"Okay, well, maybe I'll be different. Go ahead. Give it your best shot."

Leah started by kissing Chris hard on the mouth. She tasted herself on her tongue and her arousal grew. She placed a hand on one of Chris's breasts and kneaded it gently. She took her hard nipple between her fingers and twisted and tugged on it.

"You're off to a good start," Chris said.

"Good. I'm glad you like it."

She kissed down Chris's neck and chest until she replaced her fingers with her mouth. She sucked hard on the nipple, pulling it as far into her mouth as she could.

"Easy," Chris said. "Don't pull it off."

Damn. She needed to start easy and if they wanted more they'd tell her, right?

"Sorry."

"It's okay. Just be gentle, okay?"

"I will."

She lowered her mouth again.

"No. Not that one. I think it's too sore now. You can try the other one."

Gently, Leah took the nipple in her mouth and ran her tongue over it.

"That's it," Chris said. "Much better."

Leah kept at it until the draw to move lower became too much for her. She kissed down Chris's rippled belly until her scent wafted up to greet her. She needed to taste her, to eat her, to please her with her mouth.

She climbed between Chris's legs and spread them wide. She gazed at the beauty that was Chris. She smelled delicious, and Leah was sure she would taste divine. She lowered her head and ran her tongue over the length of her. She was so wet and so warm that Leah almost forgot her instructions and lost herself in her. Instead, she took a deep breath and made her alphabet.

"That feels great, but I need you to concentrate on one area," Chris said.

Leah buried her tongue inside her and licked her satin walls. She stretched her tongue as far as it would go. Then she licked to her clit so she could use her fingers inside.

"Jesus Christ," Chris said. And not in a good way. "How long are your nails? I think you cut me."

Leah slipped her hand out and showed Chris her nails. She'd always kept them longish, but never thought that might be a problem.

"Those things are talons. Never mind. I'm through here."

"Please. Let me try to please you with just my mouth."

"No. The mood is gone. I'm sorry, but Jesus, that hurt."

"I'm so sorry."

"Me, too. I thought we might have a little fun. Well, we did at first anyway, didn't we?"

Leah nodded as she watched Chris get dressed. She put on a robe and walked her to the door.

"Thanks for the memories," Chris said. "And for Christ's sake. Cut your nails."

Leah closed the door behind her. It was still early. She went to her dressing table and got her fingernail clippers. She almost cried as she cut her beautiful nails short. She took the polish off and climbed into bed, ready for the night to be over.

❖

Dillon arrived at work the next morning to find Leah already there.

"I thought you were going to be late. What happened? How'd it go last night?"

"Not good."

"No? Seriously? Maybe these random women just aren't right for you."

"No. I've learned something from each of them, I think."

"What did you learn from Chris?"

Leah held her hands up for Dillon to inspect them.

"Leah! What have you done with your nails?"

"Apparently, they were talons and caused harm when inserted in a woman."

Dillon sat at her desk and stared at Leah. She knew how proud Leah had always been of her long, polished nails. She looked naked without them. She could see how they could hurt, but there were ways of getting around that.

"You don't have to put your fingers in a woman to please her."

"I know."

"Leah. I'm so sorry."

"It's okay." Leah's smile looked forced. "Lesson learned. Onward and upward."

"No, it's not okay. You look pained. Those nails were your pride and joy."

"But they weren't conducive to good lovemaking, so they had to go. Just another lesson I've learned."

"Look. You've already hooked up with three women. Don't you think that's about enough?"

Leah shook her head.

"Nope. Not until I please one. Or more. I've got a lot to learn, my friend. Trust me."

"I just think you're hookin' up with the wrong women."

"I don't. Each one has taught me something valuable. Even if the first two contradicted each other."

"And that's another thing I keep telling you. Pleasing one woman doesn't mean you can please them all."

"And just how many women have you been with that you weren't able to please?" Leah said.

"That's not fair."

"Why? Because the answer is zero, right? You're a natural, aren't you?"

"I'm not having this conversation with you."

Dillon didn't want to talk about the women she'd been with with Leah. Mostly because at that stage in her life, Leah was the only woman she wanted to be with. The rest didn't matter. None of them did. Not even Lucinda. She shook her head. She didn't want to think of her. Not now. Not ever. She was ancient history.

"What's going on in that head of yours?" Leah said.

"Nothing. Nothing at all. I'm just tired of having this conversation with you. I think if you find the right woman, sex will be right, too."

"Come on. That's not true and you know it. Sueann was the right woman for me. Still is. And sex wasn't right. That's why I'm using this app now."

"How can you be so sure she was the right one?"

"Everyone said we made the perfect couple. We were happy. We enjoyed each other. Except, apparently, the sex. So I'll learn all I can and when I can make her scream my name I'll look her up and we'll get back together."

Dillon wanted to punch something. She didn't like the idea of any other woman screaming Leah's name. The thought made her nauseous. But if Leah was still determined to go through with this, at least she could be there to check out the women. It was pretty much all she could do.

"I'm going to start getting the bar ready to open," she said.

"I've got the deposit ready. I'll head into town and buy stuff for the lunch rush. Can you think of anything else we need?"

Just you. But she couldn't say that.

"Nope. I think we're good."

"Okay. I'll see you in a bit."

Left alone to her own thoughts, Dillon got more and more depressed. She hated the position she was in with Leah. But she knew once you entered the friend zone, you were stuck. And that's where she was. Firmly. And as her best friend, she was expected to be supportive. Maybe, just maybe, if she was more supportive, Leah would see how good she was for her. The thought brightened her up a little bit anyway. She set about getting ready to open for business.

Dillon worked the lunch rush alongside their top bartender, Wynona. She was young but great with people, drinks, and money. They'd never had a problem with her. She'd been with them for several years, and Dillon was grateful to have her working with her during the rush and after, when several women stayed behind to drink their afternoon away.

Leah came out of the office as tne lunch rush ended. She was great with books and was easy on the eyes, but she wasn't good during crowded times. She tended to get flustered. Dillon didn't mind, though. She had no problem working during the busy times. And Leah would work behind the bar in between lunch and happy hour. She and Wynona got along very well. Everything worked like a finely oiled machine. Dillon was proud of them all.

"Hey Dillon?" Wynona said after the rush was over.

"Yeah?"

"Can I talk to you? In the office, I mean?"

"Sure. You can handle things, can't you, Leah?"

"No problem. This is my kind of crowd."

They laughed and Dillon held the office door open for Wynona to enter.

"What's up?" she said.

Wynona handed her a piece of paper.

"I'm giving my notice."

"You're what? I thought you were happy here. What is it? Do you need more money? What?"

"No. I just got offered a job in my field. Remember, I did go to college and didn't study mixology." She laughed. "Look, I've really enjoyed my time here, and I want to leave with no hard feelings."

"No. No hard feelings at all. I'm very happy for you. When do you start your new job?"

"Next week. I'm really sorry for the short notice."

"That's okay. Really. We'll just shift the schedule around a bit until we hire someone new. Damn, we're going to miss you, Wy."

"I'll miss you, too. I do hope I'm still allowed to come visit sometime?"

"You'd better."

They hugged and left the office to find Leah in a deep conversation with a patron.

"You two solving world problems?" Dillon said.

"Nothing like that. Just talking baseball," the patron said.

"Like Leah understands that?"

"She's trying to teach me." Leah laughed. "So what was that private convo about?"

Dillon handed Leah Wynona's notice.

"Oh no," Leah said. "What are we going to do without her?"

"We just have to hire someone new."

"And until then?"

"We work our asses off."

"Great."

CHAPTER FIVE

Dillon spent the better part of the next week working on an ad for the paper and flyers to post around town in hopes of finding a new bartender sooner rather than later.

"Why has it taken you so long to do that?" Leah said Friday.

"Because I want it to be perfect. We have to interview these people and I only want serious people to apply. We have to work with whoever we choose."

"I get that. But still, how hard can it be to find a bartender?"

"I don't know if you get how much Wy did for us. We're going to be lost without her. And her shoes are pretty big to fill."

Leah plopped into her desk chair.

"So, is now not a good time to talk to you?"

"What about?"

"I have a date set up for tonight."

Dillon cringed inside. Here they went again.

"Okay. So?"

"So will you hang out a little past five? I want you to meet her, as usual."

"A little past five? That's awfully early. You think she's going to give you a twelve-hour lesson?"

"Actually, she wants to take me to dinner before. Kind of get to know me, I guess."

"Ah. To make sure you're not the serial killer or anything, huh?"

Leah laughed.

"Yeah. Something like that I guess."

"Sure. No problem. Who's the lucky lady this week?"

"Her name is Cindy."

She handed the phone to Dillon to look at.

"She's cute."

"I think so. She looks fairly harmless."

"I don't know though. You've got to watch out for those redheads. They can be pretty feisty."

"I don't think I'd mind feisty."

"Leah, let me ask you something. So far you've gone on how many of these dates?"

"Three."

"And have you really learned anything?"

"Dillon, don't start with me again. I'm not going to quit until I'm an expert lover. I've made up my mind."

"But tell me what you've learned. Never mind. I don't want to know. If you think it's important I'll support you. I try to be supportive, but sometimes it's hard."

"And I don't understand what the big deal is. You'd think it would be easy to support your so-called best friend."

"So-called? What's that supposed to mean? You know you're my best friend. You have been for years and will continue to be so. I don't know what I'd do without you."

Leah leaned over and hugged her.

"You'll never have to find out. I promise."

Dillon tried to focus on her words, but all she could think about was how soft Leah's breasts were against her neck. She wanted to turn around and bury her face between them. She took a deep breath.

"That's good to know. So I think I've got the ad perfected. I'm going to go online to post it in the local paper. You want to take some fliers to the university and post some there?"

"Do we really want college students? Are you sure about this?"

"I'm sure. We might need two or three part-timers to cover Wy's shifts. Unless we find one perfect one. But I'm not holding out much hope for that."

"Right. Okay. I'll go post the fliers. Then I'll head home to shower and get ready to meet Cindy."

"Sounds good. I'll help Wy with the afternoon crowd and I'll stick around to meet your date."

"Thanks. See you in a few."

Dillon was thankful for a hectic lunch rush. She kept the beer and drinks flowing and made sure the food was served in a timely manner. She took a few minutes to hang back and watch Wynona do her thing. She was such a natural. How was Dillon ever going to find a replacement for her?

The rush also kept her mind off her impending meeting with this Cindy person. Yet another anonymous woman who'd be taking Leah to bed. Dillon wondered briefly if the women were pleasing Leah or if it was simply Leah's job to please them. She shook her head. It was not something she could bear to think about.

"You with us, boss?" Wy said.

"Sure. Sorry. Why?"

"You're lagging behind. I could use your help."

"Okay. Sorry I spaced there for a moment."

"No worries. Just help me now, okay?"

Dillon got through the rest of lunch, and finally, the pace slowed as the regulars left to get back to work. She loved her regulars and loved her job. They'd told them Wy was leaving, and Dillon looked over to see Wy's tip jar was filled to the brim. And she still had four hours to go.

"Damn, woman. You're rakin' in the money today."

"They're going to miss me. I get that. I'll miss them, too. But it's my time to move on. I have to say, though, I don't think any job I have will measure up to the fun I've had working here."

"That's nice of you to say."

"I mean it. This place is great. And you and Leah have been awesome to work for."

"And speaking of work, I have some to do in the office. I'll be there if you need me. If not, I'll resurface around happy hour."

"Okay. See you then."

Dillon went into the office and closed the door. The room smelled faintly of Leah's perfume. It was a clean scent that made her whole body come alive every time she smelled it. She buried her head in her hands. This business Leah was doing would be the death of her yet. She had to put an end to it. But how?

Shaking herself from her self-pity, she went on several job posting sites and posted the bartender position. Several of their current employees had volunteered to step up and take on more shifts. For this she was grateful, but she knew it would be piecemeal and she didn't like that. She wanted a full-time day bartender. She wanted Wy to stay.

Soon it was three o'clock and time to help with happy hour. The crowd wasn't crazy, and she was just pretty much there to help out if Wy needed her. She served a few people, then positioned herself on a bar stool on the other side of the bar to watch television until she was needed again. She heard a voice next to her.

"So, Wy's really leaving, huh?"

Dillon turned to see Stephanie, one of their regulars, leaning on the bar beside her. Stephanie looked to be in her late twenties. She was tall, almost as tall as Dillon, and had long dark hair and blue eyes. She was very good-looking and always flirtatious. Dillon enjoyed her very much.

"Yep. She's taking a real job."

"What are you going to do? No offense, but she pretty much runs this place."

Dillon laughed.

"None taken. You're right. And I don't know what we're going to do. We're looking for someone to take over for her."

"I might know someone."

"Yeah? Who?"

"Me."

"But I thought you worked at the mill. Oh no. Don't tell me you got caught in the layoffs going around."

"I did indeed. Office staff was not immune. I used to tend bar while I was in college. It's been a few years, but I bet I could get the hang of it again."

"Hey, Wy?" Dillon called out.

"What's up, boss?"

"Get Stephanie here an apron. Shadow her, but I want her to try her hand at bartending this afternoon."

"Are you serious?" both women said together.

Dillon laughed again.

"Very. But, Stephanie, if it doesn't work out, no hard feelings, okay?"

"Fair enough."

"We do have the Bartender's Bible here." Wy held up a little black book. "It'll help you if you get stumped."

"Will I get demerits if I use it?" she asked Dillon.

"Not at all. As long as you're not overly slow about it. Slow is okay as you learn and get the hang of where everything is here, but overly slow won't work. And Wy is here today to help you out."

"Most excellent."

She went behind the bar. She looked natural there. And hot. She was a very attractive woman. The first customer came in and ordered a Seven and Seven. Easy-peasy. She mixed it in no time and set it down. She turned to Wy.

"I don't know how much everything is except my glass of white wine."

"We keep a list over by the cash register. Come on. I'll show you."

But the patron had already left six dollars on the bar and walked away.

"Congratulations," Wy said. "Your first tip."

Dillon smiled. This just might work.

She was sitting with Stephanie after her shift when Leah walked in.

"Hi, Leah," Stephanie said. "You look nice."

"Thanks. I have a date."

"Excellent."

"Hey, Leah, I'd like you to meet our new bartender."

"Already? Who?"

"Stephanie."

"What?" She laughed. "When did this happen?"

"This afternoon. She got laid off at the mill and has some bartending experience, so I let her try during happy hour. She was fantastic."

"That's awesome," Leah said. "So my time traipsing around campus today was all for naught?"

"I'm afraid so. That reminds me. I have to cancel our ad in the paper. We don't need to be charged if we don't need it to be run."

"True."

"I'll go do that right now."

Leah put her hand on Dillon's arm. Dillon felt the heat burning into her skin.

"What's up?"

"You can't go right now. Cindy is due any minute."

"Cindy?" Stephanie said.

"My date. And I want Dillon to feel her out for me."

"I guess as long as she doesn't feel her up you're okay, huh?" Stephanie laughed.

Leah laughed with her. She'd always liked Stephanie and was looking forward to having her on staff at The Kitty. Plus, she was easy on the eyes, which the customers would love.

"Oh shit," Leah said. "I think she's here."

"Is this a blind date?" Stephanie said.

"Something like that."

"Where is she?" Dillon said.

"There. Just inside the front door."

They were both looking in the mirror.

"Looks like her to me," Dillon said.

"Well, I'll let you two do what you've got to do. I'll see you all on Monday."

"Good-bye. And thanks."

They watched in the mirror as the tall redhead approached them. Leah turned around and smiled at her. It was a genuine smile, because she was ready to try again. She felt like this time she'd really be able to take a woman to an orgasm.

"Cindy?" she said.

"That's me." Cindy smiled back at her. "How are you?"

"I'm great. And you?"

"Can't complain. I've got a hot date with a lovely woman tonight."

Leah blushed.

"Cindy, this is my best friend, Dillon. Dillon, meet Cindy."

"How do you do?" Dillon said and extended a hand.

"Nice to meet you. So are you the protective friend looking out for Leah?"

"Something like that."

"Well, you needn't worry. I'm the perfect gentlebutch."

"I hope so."

"I promise. Leah will be very well taken care of." She winked.

Something passed over Dillon's face that Leah couldn't read. Oh well. It wasn't important. She was ready to get dinner over with so she and Cindy could get down to fun and games.

"Shall we?" she said.

"Certainly." Cindy placed her hand in the small of Leah's back and guided her out the door. The summer air was warm, and Leah lifted her face to smell the fragrant flowers growing around the bar.

"I love this time of year," she said.

"It gets a little too hot for me. And I can't be out in the sun, obviously, but for now, it's beautiful."

"So where are we going for dinner?"

"A little hole in the wall. You want me to drive?"

"I'll follow you."

Cindy arched an eyebrow at her but agreed.

Leah followed her to a nondescript looking building on the west side of town, not far from her house. She wondered why she'd never been there before. She parked her car next to Cindy's and they walked in together.

"What's good here?" Leah said.

"Everything. They're known for their steak and lobster, though. I highly recommend it. It's what I'll be having."

Leah closed her menu.

"Then that's what I'll have as well. So tell me about yourself, Cindy. Your profile just said you like fast cars and good women."

Cindy laughed.

"I actually race on the NASCAR circuit. Though you'll not have heard of me, since I'm not one of the top names. Yet."

"Wow. That's ambitious."

"I love it. I love the speed, the competition. It suits me. Now tell me, Leah, are you a good woman?"

"I like to think so."

"Just not in bed, though, huh? I must say, your profile intrigued me. I wasn't sure what to expect when I met you. And, for the record, you profile picture doesn't do you justice."

Leah blushed.

"Well, thank you. I'll have to find a more suitable one, I guess."

"You really should."

They sipped their drinks in silence before Cindy spoke again.

"So what do you mean exactly that you're not good in bed?"

"I don't seem to be able to make a woman climax."

Cindy raised her eyebrows.

"Seriously? That surprises me. You can come though, right?"

"Oh yeah." Leah laughed. "I have no problem in that department."

"Good. Well, we'll work on what we can and see if we can change your record tonight."

Leah sighed.

"I sure hope so. I'm getting frustrated."

"I can only imagine. Pleasing a woman is one of the greatest joys on earth."

"And that I can only imagine."

"So what are your hang-ups?"

They were silent as the waitress set down their dinners.

"Hang-ups? I don't know that I really have any. I try my best, but I always end up crashing and burning."

"Okay. Well, eat up. We've got some work to do."

After dinner, Cindy followed Leah to her house. Leah had had several glasses of wine and was feeling very relaxed. She was highly attracted to Cindy and was ready to have her way with her.

Cindy pulled Leah to her in the living room.

"So, how are you at kissing?"

"It's hit or miss."

"Really? Tell me you don't stop to think what you're doing."

"I've been told I use too much tongue. Then that I don't use enough. I told you, it's frustrating."

"Okay, Well, I'm not huge on tongue, so it's okay if you don't use a lot, okay?"

Leah nodded as she looked into Cindy's eyes. She felt herself getting lost in them. If Cindy didn't kiss her soon, she didn't know what she'd do. But she didn't have to wait. Cindy lowered her mouth and claimed hers in a deep, passionate kiss. Leah was even more lightheaded when the kiss ended.

"That was nice. I've wanted to do that all night," Cindy said. "So far, so good. Are you nervous? Aroused? Talk to me."

"Very aroused," Leah said. "And somewhat nervous. I mean, once you're through with me, I'll be a nervous wreck."

"Who says I'm going to take you first?"

"Please. Dear God, please. I need you."

Cindy laughed. It was a deep, throaty sound that made Leah's lower lips swell.

"Actually, I was just teasing. I wouldn't have it any other way. Let's get you to bed before I explode all over your living room."

They walked down the hall arm in arm until they reached Leah's bedroom. There, Cindy kissed her again, and Leah felt her toes curl in response. She pulled Cindy down to her and kissed her as hard as she could, conscious of how much tongue she was using.

"You kiss just fine," Cindy said when she finally broke the kiss. "Now let's get naked. You first. Undress slowly. I like to watch."

Leah turned around so Cindy could unzip her dress. As it fell to the floor and she stepped out of her slip, Cindy let out a low wolf whistle.

"No panties. I like it."

Leah unhooked her bra and stood self-consciously for Cindy's inspection.

"My God. You're a work of art," Cindy said. "Now lie down. I'll undress and join you."

Leah watched Cindy strip out of her clothes and marveled at the toned body underneath. She obviously hit the gym often. And Leah was appreciative of that.

When Cindy climbed up onto the bed, she slid on top of Leah and kissed her hard again while she drew her knee up to press into Leah's center.

"Damn. You're so wet," she said.

"I need you, Cindy. Please. Take me."

"Gladly."

Cindy lowered her mouth to tenderly suck on Leah's nipples. Leah felt them harden at the attention they were receiving. They felt like little pebbles on the ends of her breasts. She was so turned on, she didn't know how much longer she could wait for Cindy to taste her.

But Cindy didn't taste her. She skimmed her hand down Leah's body until she was where her knee had just been. She easily slipped her fingers inside. Leah arched to take her in. She gyrated all over to make sure all her favorite spots were hit. When Cindy slid her fingers to her clit, Leah closed her eyes and felt every muscle in her body tense. She was tense only briefly as the orgasms hit her and she rode one after another until she was a pool of nothingness.

CHAPTER SIX

When Leah had come to her senses, she realized Cindy was lying there, legs spread, waiting her turn. And Leah couldn't wait to taste her, to please her. She kissed her hard on her mouth, loving the way their tongues danced together. She kissed down her chest to her nipples. She gently loved on them with her mouth and tongue. Cindy was breathing heavily and moaning slightly. Leah smiled to herself. She was on the right track.

Leah kissed lower, down Cindy's stomach.

"Uh-uh," Cindy said.

"What?" Leah looked up at her.

"I don't do oral. It doesn't work for me. Not giving or receiving. Use your hand."

Leah was flustered. So far, she'd tried to learn how to please a woman with her mouth. She hadn't used only her hand. She took a deep breath.

"Okay."

She slid her hand down between Cindy's open legs. She was wet and swollen. And oh-so warm. Leah felt her own clit swell again at the feel of her. She could smell her and wanted to see her, to taste her, but she couldn't so she just felt around down there to try to figure out what went where.

She slipped her fingers inside and pulled them back out. She thrust them in deeper and Cindy raised her ass off the bed to greet her. Leah hoped she was close. She looked at Cindy. Her eyes were closed, her head thrashing back and forth on the pillow. Leah withdrew her fingers and dragged them to her clit.

"That's it baby," Cindy said. "Put one finger on either side and drag them slowly up and down."

Leah did just that. She concentrated on keeping her fingers from sliding all over the place since Cindy was so slick.

"Now press a little harder, but don't stop. Whatever you do, don't stop."

Leah was feeling hopeful and she added a little pressure. Cindy was pumping up and down in time with Leah's strokes.

"Oh, yes. Oh, dear God, yes," Cindy said. She kept moving and Leah kept stroking. Just when Leah wondered if anything was going to happen, Cindy stiffened, cried out, then collapsed on the bed.

"Did we do it?" Leah said.

"Oh yeah, we did it. You were amazing, Leah. I don't know how anyone could tell you you're not good in bed. You follow instructions well and seem to know what you're doing with those magical fingers of yours."

"Thank you," Leah said. "Thank you so much."

"Thank *you*. Because, believe me, the pleasure was all mine."

"I don't know. I rather enjoyed myself, too."

"Excellent. Now, lie back. It's time for me to reward you."

Leah was happy to oblige. She was so excited from playing with Cindy, and she thought she'd have to take care of herself when Cindy left. But if Cindy was offering, who was she to say no?

She felt Cindy enter her and moaned. She hadn't been expecting that so soon. But that was fine. Cindy felt amazing inside her and she arched off the bed to encourage her to go deeper. Cindy did just that. Every thrust seemed to push her deeper and deeper inside Leah. Leah was groaning in pleasure when Cindy slipped her hand over her clit and rubbed it until Leah felt her whole world quake. When she was on solid ground again, she looked up to see Cindy smiling at her again.

"What?" Leah said.

"Nothing. You're just so damned fun. You ready to get some sleep?"

Sleep? So she was planning on spending the night? Leah wasn't sure what to say.

"It is okay if I sleep over, isn't it? Or are you going to kick me out?"

When she put it that way, Leah couldn't bring herself to ask her to leave.

"Let's get some sleep," she finally said.

She lay down and Cindy snuggled in behind her. They fell sound asleep.

Leah woke up the next morning to Cindy's fingers on her tender clit. At first it hurt a little, but soon the pleasure overtook the pain and Leah was screaming Cindy's name again.

Cindy lay back and spread her legs.

"My turn. Work your magic. Just like last night."

Leah did the same thing she'd done the night before, and she once again took Cindy to several orgasms. Cindy lay there with her eyes closed. Leah rested her head on her chest. It felt nice. Until Cindy spoke.

"Okay. Now it's time for me to get going."

"Okay. Well, thank you. It's been a lot of fun."

"Yes, it has. Keep your eye on the NASCAR rankings. You just might see me in the top numbers someday."

"I will."

She walked Cindy to the door, kissed her good-bye and went back to bed. She had made a woman come. She couldn't get the smile off her face. She slept for a few more hours, then got up and took a long, hot bath. She was quite sore, but ready to try again the next weekend if someone contacted her. Making one woman come was incredible, but she needed to make several do it in order to feel confident.

She got out of her bath and heard her phone ringing.

"Hello?"

"Hey, kiddo," Dillon said. "How are you this morning?"

"I'm fantastic."

"You are, huh? Dare I ask why?"

"I made Cindy come last night."

There was silence on the other end of the line.

"Dillon? Are you there?"

"Huh? Yeah. That's great. So, you've done it now. You can quit using that stupid app?"

"Oh no. Cindy was just one woman. I need to please many."

"Leah, I think you've proven your point."

"What? Have you not been listening to me? Do you not understand how important this is for me?"

"I know you wanted to learn how to please a woman. Now you have."

"It's still not the same, though."

"What's not the same?"

"Well, if you must know, Cindy doesn't like oral, so I had to use my fingers."

Dillon closed her eyes tight and tried to get the visual out of her mind. The last thing she needed were details of Leah's encounters. She didn't want to think of Leah going down on another woman or touching one intimately. She shuddered. Her appetite was gone, but she knew she needed food and assumed Leah would, too.

"Okay. Well, the reason I called was to see if you wanted to have lunch."

"Lunch would be great. I'm famished. Can we do Mexican?"

"Sure. Whatever you want." It would always be whatever Leah wanted. If only she would want Dillon. That would make life perfect.

"Okay. You want to pick me up? I can be ready in fifteen."

"Yeah. I'll leave now."

Dillon slipped her phone in her pocket. Why did she put herself through this misery? Because she was crazy about Leah and wanted to spend more time with her. Even if that time meant hearing about her in bed with other women. She must be a masochist to set herself up for that kind of pain, but so be it. Lunch with Leah was set now. She couldn't very well call and say she'd changed her mind.

She picked Leah up and drove her to her favorite restaurant. The wait staff knew them by name. They greeted them and took them to their favorite table. It sat by a plate glass window with a beautiful view of the courtyard. Dillon had started to relax and was ready to enjoy a fine meal with Leah.

"So how are you today?" Leah said.

"I'm great. No complaints. Ready to have a weekend away from the bar."

"Yeah. Sorry about having you there to meet women with me on weekends. It's just that that's the way it usually works out."

"And I don't mind," Dillon lied. "It's just nice to get away from there for a couple of days. You know, treat it like a regular job."

"Yeah. I can see that. So, what are you doing this weekend?"

"I don't know. Stephanie mentioned a softball game. I might go check that out."

"Oh. When is that?"

Dillon checked her watch.

"In an hour."

"I want to go. Can I go with?"

"Sure. It'll be fun."

They ate their lunch and paid their tab. Dillon checked her watch again.

"The game should have started by now. We should drive over."

"Sounds great."

More time with Leah sounded great. They drove to the softball complex on the south side of town. There were three games going at once.

"I wonder which field they're on," Dillon said.

Just then she heard someone call her name. She looked over to see Stephanie waving from the field closest to them. They walked over and sat in the bleachers. Dillon was struck once again at how beautiful Stephanie was. She was lithe and lean and built to play first base. Which she did very well. She was even easier on the eyes than Dillon had previously realized. She wondered briefly if she was seeing anyone. Surely she was.

The game went on until Stephanie's team won six to four. It was a fun game to watch. Stephanie came over to sit in the stands with Dillon and Leah.

"Good game," Dillon said.

"Thanks. It was fun."

"So, Dryer's Gas sponsors you? I heard they were going out of business," Leah said.

"They are. We might not be able to finish the season if we don't find another sponsor."

"Maybe we could sponsor you," Dillon said. She didn't miss the look Leah shot her. "Why don't you find out what's entailed and Leah and I can talk it over."

"That would be great."

"We should get going," Leah said.

"I'm going to try to get the team to go to The Kitty to celebrate. You guys want to join us?"

"I need to get home," Leah said.

"I'll join you. Just let me drop Leah off."

Once in the truck, Dillon turned to face Leah.

"Okay. What is it?"

"What's what?"

"The coolness. You were like ice back there."

"I own the bar, too, you know. You hired her without checking with me and now you're talking about sponsoring them."

"I said we'd talk it over."

"Not before I shot daggers at you."

Dillon had to admit it was true.

"Okay. I'm sorry. I'll try to remember to consult with you in the future. But you've been pretty busy lately with your own endeavors."

"Not at the expense of the bar."

"True. Look, kiddo. I'm sorry."

Leah seemed to melt a little bit.

"Okay. And maybe I overreacted a little. But let's just work as a team, okay?"

"You got it. So what do you think of sponsoring the team?"

"We need to see what it entails. If we can afford it, I say we consider it."

So she still wouldn't say okay. What was up with her? Dillon couldn't worry about it at the moment. As much as she'd been looking forward to a full weekend away from the bar, the idea of partying with a softball team suddenly appealed to her. She dropped Leah off at her house.

"Enjoy the rest of your weekend," she said.

"You, too."

She watched Leah until she let herself into her house. She was sorry that Leah didn't go to the bar with her, but she wouldn't let her dampen her mood. She drove to The Kitty, parked in the back and let herself in the delivery door. The jukebox was rockin' and the women from the team were standing around it singing and dancing. Some had brought girlfriends, some had even brought boyfriends, but the mood was lively and fun.

Dillon helped herself to a beer then walked over to watch the celebration from just outside the circle. She couldn't help but smile. This group was in a rowdy mood and would likely spend a nice chunk of change there. Life was good.

She looked around for Stephanie and saw her coming from the restroom.

"You made it," Stephanie said.

"I did. Thanks for bringing the group here. I'd like to buy you a couple of pitchers, if you think that would be okay."

"I think we'd love that."

Dillon went back to the bar and ordered two pitchers and fresh glasses. Stephanie came over to help her carry the glasses.

"This is really nice of you," she said.

"Well, I appreciate the business."

"It's nice to have a place to come to after games. We've gone to other bars, but they just didn't feel right. Maybe this feels better because I work here now."

"Maybe. Whatever the reason, I'm glad you're here."

Stephanie smiled broadly.

"Me too. Now come on. Let's dance."

Dillon wanted to decline, but Stephanie had her hand and was dragging her to the center of the circle. She took a drink of beer and set her bottle on the table. She moved to the music, which was fast and loud. She could barely hear herself think, but that was okay. Time not to think about Leah was just what she needed.

The song ended and Dillon grabbed her bottle and escaped the circle before Stephanie could make her dance again. She moved to the bar and sat on a stool facing the group. A woman broke apart from the group and approached her.

"You own this place, huh?" she said.

"That I do. Well, I co-own it with my best friend."

"Where is she?"

"She couldn't make it."

"Too bad. This could be the party of the century."

"I sure hope so."

"So I saw you there dancing, but then you were gone. What happened?"

"I'm not much of a dancer."

"I saw you moving. You looked good to me."

"Well, thank you, but it's not my forte."

"So, you won't dance again with me this time?"

"No, thanks. But I'll buy you a drink," Dillon said.

"Thanks, but I'm sticking to beer."

"Then I'll buy you a beer."

"That would be great. My name's Josie, by the way."

Dillon smiled.

"I'm Dillon."

"Nice to meet you."

"Likewise."

Dillon ordered Josie a beer and they sat chatting until Stephanie walked up.

"You sure disappeared off that dance floor quickly. I didn't even have a chance to ask you for another one."

"I'm really not much of a dancer, like I was telling your friend Josie here."

"Nonsense. You did fine out there."

Dillon laughed.

"Thank you, but I know I can't dance."

"Okay, well, you have other talents."

"Oh yeah?" Josie arched an eyebrow. "And what might those be?"

"She owns a great bar and, so far, has proven to be an awesome boss."

"You've only worked for me for half a shift."

"Still. I enjoyed it."

"Good. I'm glad. I'm really happy to have you working here. So, I bought Josie a beer. Can I buy you a glass of wine?"

"Sure. Thanks." She took the bar stool on the other side of Dillon, so Dillon was seated between Josie and herself.

"You both played great games today," Dillon said and raised her bottle. "Here's to excellent wins."

"Indeed," they said in unison as they all clinked their glassware together.

"It was a lot of fun," Josie said.

"Yeah. You guys looked like you were having a good time."

A silence fell over them and it soon grew uncomfortable. The music blared in the background and people were still yelling, trying to talk over it, but the silence between the three of them was awkward. Dillon struggled to find something to say. She felt a hostility between Josie and Stephanie that she didn't understand. She stood.

"I think I'll head out now. You kids have fun."

They each placed a hand on one of Dillon's arms.

"No," they said. "Don't go."

"The party is just warming up," Stephanie said.

"Yeah. You don't want to leave now," Josie said.

Dillon sat back down and signaled the bartender for another beer.

"Okay. I'll stay. But you girls have to play nice."

"It's the only way I know to play," Josie said.

Dillon didn't miss Stephanie rolling her eyes. She had to laugh. She really liked Stephanie. Josie seemed nice, too, but Stephanie had been a patron at her bar for years and was now an employee, so Dillon liked her more.

"Please come dance some more," Stephanie said.

"Yeah. I want a chance to dance with you, too."

Dillon took a long pull off her beer and allowed herself to be led back to the floor, resigning herself to dance the night away.

CHAPTER SEVEN

Monday morning, Dillon was setting the bar up for opening when Leah came in.

"Hey, kiddo. How are you this morning?"

"I'm great. How are you?"

"Not bad. I'm glad you're in a good mood. You seemed kind of upset Saturday."

"Upset? Me? No. At least not that I can remember. I thought I was in a great mood because of my time with Cindy."

The mention of Cindy made Dillon's stomach roil. She so wished she could block out certain conversations she and Leah had had recently. Especially those about her oral talents versus non-oral talents. Those were the last things Dillon wanted to hear about.

"So any other dates lined up?"

"Yes. As a matter of fact, I'm meeting a woman here tonight after work."

"You are, huh?"

"Yes, I am. Her name in Joni, and she's looks like she'll know what she's doing."

She handed Dillon her phone.

Dillon took in the tall, dark, butch-looking woman. She was filled with jealousy. Yet another anonymous woman would be sharing Leah's bed. She hated the thought.

"She looks okay." She handed the phone back to Leah.

"Okay? She's way hot. I can't wait to meet her."

"So, how late do I have to stay here tonight?"

"Only until seven?" Leah said hopefully.

"Seven? Dang. Okay. For you. But only because you're my best friend."

"Thanks." Leah stood on her tiptoes and kissed Dillon's cheek. Dillon felt the heat of it sear through her body.

Soon, the bar was ready to open and Stephanie walked in. She looked especially stunning. Dillon figured that was because she'd never seen her first thing in the morning before. She smelled fresh and clean, and Dillon actually felt herself getting wet. She shook it off.

"You look great this morning," Dillon said.

"Thanks. I'm ready for my first full day of work. I hope I can cut it."

"I doubt there'll be any problem. And I'm here to help out."

"Great. Thanks."

Leah came out of the office.

"Hi, Stephanie."

"Hi, Leah. How are you?"

"I'm good. Thanks. And you?"

"Ready to rock and roll."

Leah smiled.

"Excellent. I'm going to run some errands. I need to do a bank deposit and pick up things for the lunch rush. I'll be back. Don't let Dillon bully you."

Stephanie looked at Dillon, then back to Leah.

"I'll try not to, but she is the boss, after all."

"So am I," Leah said.

"Oh, yeah. I know."

"Good."

Leah left and Stephanie turned to Dillon.

"Does she not like me or something?"

"No. It's not that," Dillon said. "She's just kind of upset that I hired you without consulting her. She would have agreed to it, of course. And she's happy to have you here, but she's mad at me for overstepping my place. We both own the bar and I should have talked it over with her."

"But she wasn't even here then."

"I know. Just don't you worry, okay? We're both thrilled to have you working for us."

"Thanks."

"Now, it's time to open, so I'll do it, but I want you to follow me and learn what every step is, okay?"

"Okay."

Stephanie followed behind Dillon as she turned on each neon light, opened the drapes, and put the chairs and stools on the floor.

"That was pretty easy."

"Yep. Ronnie will be in any minute now to prep the kitchen."

"I have to say, I'm happy that I don't have to cook."

"I can't promise you'll never have to, but for now, you don't."

"So, what do we do now?"

"We wait. Martha should be here for her Bloody Mary any time now. And some of the other older, retired women should wander in after her. So you'll just have to mix drinks and be charming."

"They're not going to be happy to have a new bartender, are they?" Stephanie said.

"I don't know. They loved Wynona. That's for sure. But you'll win them over, I'm sure."

Right on cue, a short, stocky woman with short gray hair walked in.

"Good morning, Martha," Dillon said.

"Hey, Dillon."

"Martha, this is our new bartender, Stephanie. You're going to love her."

"We'll see," Martha said. "It depends on how good of a Bloody Mary she makes."

Dillon fought the urge to supervise Stephanie's mixing. She trusted her. Stephanie placed the drink in front of Martha who took a sip.

"Damn. That's good. Welcome aboard."

"Thanks."

The rest of the day went smoothly, and once five o'clock rolled around, Dillon offered to buy Stephanie a glass of wine.

"That would be great. Thanks. Should I get used to this?"

Dillon laughed.

"Not necessarily. I like to head home after a shift and I'm sure you will, too. But today I need to hang out, so I thought I'd see if you wanted to join me."

"Why do you have to hang out?"

"Leah has another date tonight. She wants me to check her out. Not that I could do much with the woman she has a date with tonight. I think she could kick my ass."

She laughed uneasily.

"I don't think I've met a woman who could kick your ass," Stephanie said. "So, what's the deal with Leah's dates?"

"What do you mean?"

"This is the second time you've had to hang out and check them out."

"Ah. She just likes me to approve them."

"Okay."

They sat sipping their drinks. Leah came out of the office.

"I'm going to get ready for my date. I'll be back at seven."

"See you then," Dillon said.

"That's two hours from now," Stephanie said.

"Yep."

"I could be drunk if I stay that long."

"You don't have to stay that long. I only offered to buy you one drink."

"Too true. But I don't mind. I'll stick around and keep you company."

"That would be great. But I'm serious. Don't feel obligated."

"I don't. So, what about you, Dillon?"

"What about me what?"

"I've never seen you leave this bar with a woman. I've never heard rumors of you dating anyone. What's up with that? Are you just really discreet or what?"

Dillon laughed.

"No. Nothing like that. I'm just married to the bar. And that works for me."

"But don't you miss the companionship?"

"I get plenty of that here. Trust me. I'm fine. You don't have to worry about me. What about you? Never mind. I can't ask that."

"Sure you can. You're not interviewing me. I've already got the job. I haven't found Ms. Right yet. That's the reason I'm single."

"Well, good luck in your endeavors."

"Oh, I'm not really looking. I figure she'll come along when it's time. I'm not going to go out of my way to find anyone."

The next two hours flew by. Dillon found Stephanie as easy to talk to as she was to look at. She was almost sad when Leah showed up looking stunning in a dark green dress and matching pumps.

"Damn." Dillon felt her heart race. "You look amazing."

Leah blushed.

"Why thank you." She turned to Stephanie. "I didn't expect you to still be here."

"I've just been keeping Dillon company. I should go now though. I need to get some dinner before I get drunk or something."

"Thanks for hanging out with me."

"My pleasure."

Dillon watched in the mirror as she walked out of the bar. She turned her attention to Leah, who was speaking.

"You two sure are chummy," she said.

"I like her. She's a great bartender and a nice person."

"Good. I'm so glad she's working out. By the way, I spent a chunk of time today looking into sponsoring a softball team in summer league. I really think we can do it. And think of the advertising if they're all wearing our shirts."

"Excellent." Dillon grew silent. Leah looked in the mirror to see what she was looking at and saw the woman that had to be Joni. She was tall, dark, and handsome. And headed her way. She took a deep breath to steady herself then turned to face Joni.

"Hello," she said.

"Leah?"

"That's me." She tried to keep the shaking out of her voice. She was terrified of Joni and she didn't know why. Probably because she exuded confidence. Something Leah lacked completely. At least in the bedroom.

"Great. I'm so happy to meet you. I'm really looking forward to tonight."

"Me, too. Would you like a drink? I know I could use a dirty martini."

"Sure. I'll have a Vodka Collins."

"And I'll have another beer," Dillon said.

"Oh, Joni, this is my best friend, Dillon."

She watched as Dillon and Joni sized each other up. Neither seemed particularly pleased to be meeting the other.

Finally, Joni extended her hand. Dillon took it and they shook.

"Are you going with us tonight?" Joni said.

"What? No. She's just here to meet you," Leah said.

"I was just joking." Joni smiled. Finally, her façade cracked and she looked like a normal woman. Her eyes brightened and dimples showed. She was even more gorgeous, but less intimidating.

Dillon didn't say anything but ordered their drinks. When they were delivered, Joni raised hers.

"To a memorable night."

"Indeed," Leah said.

Dillon said nothing, but took a drink. Leah shot her a look, but she didn't seem to notice.

"This is a nice place. I've never been here before."

"Thanks," Dillon said. "We like it."

"Yeah? You come here often?"

"We own it," Leah said.

Joni raised her eyebrows.

"No lie? I can't believe I didn't even know it existed. How long has it been here?"

"Five years," Leah said.

"I'll have to come back some time."

"We hope you do."

Dillon threw back her head and drained her beer.

"It's time for me to hit the road. You two kids have fun tonight."

"Oh, don't worry," Joni said. "We will."

They finished their drinks.

"So, dinner first?" Joni said.

"Are you sure?"

"Sure I am. We'll go on a proper date to make sure we're even compatible to take it to the next level." She allowed her gaze to slowly roam over Leah, head to toe. "Though I have very little doubt about that."

Leah felt the heat rise to her cheeks. Damn. Joni was a brazen one. She needed to stay calm and remember everything she'd learned so far. She was sure Joni would give her instructions, too. She just told herself to keep her cool and everything would be fine.

"We can take my truck," Joni said.

"I'll follow you," Leah said. She'd felt like Joni's comment was more an instruction, but she wasn't comfortable having only one vehicle. She liked the independence having her own car gave her.

"Fine. Suit yourself."

She wasn't happy and Leah knew it. Maybe this had been a mistake. But she was so gorgeous, and she'd answered her ad. And she hadn't given Dillon any bad vibes. That was key. Dillon would get the willies if anyone was even slightly off.

"Where are we going?"

"Just follow me."

"Okay."

Leah got in her car and gripped her steering wheel. She didn't know why she was so nervous. Maybe because she'd actually pleased Cindy, so now the pressure was on to please Joni as well. Yes. That had to be it. It was all the added pressure. She followed Joni to an Italian restaurant downtown. Leah was familiar with it and the hostess greeted her by name when they walked in.

"You must come here a lot," Joni said.

"Not that often. But enough."

Joni placed her hand on Leah's upper back as they followed the hostess to their table. She waited until Leah was seated, then sat. She ordered them a bottle of wine, then sat with her hands together on the table.

"So, tell me, Leah, what's your story?"

"What do you mean?"

"You post a profile on a women's app saying you want to learn to be good in bed. How did that come about? Or did you just wake up one day and think, 'I need to learn how to fuck'?"

Leah tried not to let her shock at Joni's brashness show.

"No. It wasn't exactly like that. Though, I suppose in some ways it was."

"How so?"

"My partner of five years dumped me about six months ago and one of the main reasons she gave was that I was lousy in bed. I didn't come up with the idea of meeting women to learn from until a few weeks ago."

"Fair enough. So how many women have you met so far?"

"A few." Leah didn't feel comfortable telling her exactly how many.

"And how's your track record with them?"

Leah lowered her voice.

"I've been successful with one."

"And by successful you mean you got her off?"

Leah nodded.

"Good." Joni smiled. "So, we know there's hope for you. I have to say, you're a good-looking woman and I can't wait to get you home."

The look in her eyes was almost wolfish, and Leah worried she wouldn't be able perform under the pressure she was sure Joni would put on her. Or maybe it was the pressure she put on herself. Either way, a knot formed in her stomach as she sat looking at Joni and thinking about the night ahead.

"You look nervous," Joni said. "Here, have some more wine."

She poured another generous glass for Leah.

"Thanks. I am nervous. I always am. I mean, not being able to perform is embarrassing."

"Maybe you think about it too hard. I say relax and let it happen."

"I'll certainly try. I must say, though, you're rather intimidating."

Joni laughed. It was a deep rumble that sounded like it came from her very soul.

"I don't mean to be intimidating. I can't help my size. I'm still a woman. A woman looking for pleasure in the arms of another woman."

"And that sounds very nice."

"Good. I'm glad we agree."

They finished their dinners and another bottle of wine. Leah was feeling very mellow. She was also more aroused than she'd ever been. Why was it that each woman aroused her more than the one before? Maybe it was her imagination, but Joni had her wet and wanting her.

As soon as the front door was closed behind them, Joni gently pulled Leah to her. Leah's heart was racing. How could such a big woman be so gentle? And would she be that gentle in bed?

"So, how are you on the receiving end of things?" Joni said.

"I've got that down."

"Good." She smiled that lupine smile again. She looked like she was going to eat Leah alive. And Leah was ready for her.

Joni's gaze never wavered as she lowered her head to take Leah's lips in hers. She held Leah's gaze in hers until the last minute. Then, she closed her eyes and Leah felt her strong lips on her own. Joni ran her tongue along Leah's lips and she opened them willingly, wanting more than anything to feel Joni's tongue dance with hers.

As soon as their tongues met, Leah's knees went weak. Joni's tongue was as strong and forceful as the rest of her, demanding in its travels around Leah's mouth. She tasted of wine, and Leah ran her tongue over hers in order to taste more of her. They kissed well together, which Leah hoped boded well for later in the night.

Just when Leah thought her head would explode, Joni broke the kiss and picked her up.

"Which way to the bedroom?" Her voice was deep and sensual.

Leah could only point. She didn't trust her own voice. Joni carried her down the hall and laid her on the bed. She carefully undressed her, with Leah's help, then stood upright and shed her own clothes.

Leah felt vulnerable as she lay there exposed, waiting for Joni to take her. But it wasn't a bad sensation. She found she kind of liked it. She trusted Joni to know what she was doing. Joni lay down next to her on the bed. She kissed her hard again and ran her strong hand down her body. She paused to play with a breast. She pulled and twisted Leah's nipple before moving her hand lower. She stopped just above her curls and brought her hand back up to play with her other nipple.

"Please," Leah said. "I don't know how much teasing I can take."

"Don't you think it's fair that I tease the hell out of you?" Joni's voice was husky. "Since we don't even know if I'm going to be satisfied when this is over?"

Leah swallowed hard. Her mouth had gone dry. She needed Joni, but Joni did have a point. Joni smiled at her then and kissed down her belly. She spread her legs and took her place between them.

Her expert tongue found Leah's lips and worked its magic on them. Leah felt her move inside and ground into her face. She was close already. So close. She needed Joni to finish her off.

"Please," she said again. "Please."

Joni licked her way to Leah's nerve center and skimmed it with her tongue. Leah felt her whole world coalesce inside her. Then, with one last lick, her world splintered into a million tiny pieces.

Chapter Eight

When Leah could see straight again, she took a deep breath and silently told herself she could do this. She could please Joni. But inside, she was scared. What had she learned? Listen to your partner. Pay attention to what her body says. It sounded easy enough, but Leah was doubting herself big time when she kissed Joni.

Joni pushed Leah off her.

"The first thing you need to remember is to relax. You're wound so tight right now you're about to pop. Just relax. Take it easy and let it happen."

Leah nodded and kissed Joni's neck. She tasted good and smelled amazing. She kissed lower until she could suck one of Joni's nipples deep into her mouth. Joni moaned slightly as she arched her back, then tapped Leah's head.

"Gentle, Leah. No need to suck them off."

Frustrated, Leah collapsed onto the bed next to Joni.

"What's wrong?" Joni said.

"Everything. I don't even know why I try."

"Easy there. If you want to learn, you have to be open to instruction. You can't throw a temper tantrum every time someone corrects you."

"I'm not throwing a temper tantrum. I'm just frustrated."

"I don't understand. You wanted to learn. I'm trying to help you, but now you're getting all upset."

"I'm sorry. It's just—"

"Save it." Joni got out of bed. "We're through here."

"But I was just getting started."

"Well, the mood is gone. I'm out of here. Good luck with your quest."

Leah sat dumbfounded while she watched Joni dress and leave. Alone in her dark bedroom, she fought the burning that began behind her eyes. She took a deep breath, but soon a tear, followed by another, trickled down her cheek She lay down and hugged her pillow to her chest and sobbed herself to sleep.

She woke the next morning and asked herself if it was even worth it to keep up the lessons. Maybe she should just accept that she'd never be any good in bed. But no, she believed, deep in her heart, that she could do it. She'd gotten Cindy off, hadn't she? Joni had just been impatient. That was all. Leah would have gotten herself together and done her best to please her if given the opportunity.

Women were tricky people. She should have figured that out after Denise and Donna. But she'd learned a little with each woman she'd been with. She just needed to keep sleeping with different women until she had it down. She got out of bed and took her shower and got ready for work.

She got to the bar before Dillon and set about adding up the cash and receipts from the day before to enter them into their bookkeeping program and to prepare the cash for deposit in the bank. She was lost in her work and didn't hear Dillon come in.

She jumped when she looked up and saw Dillon leaning on the doorjamb looking at her.

"Judging from the baggy eyes, I'd say you had a good night, huh?" Dillon said.

Leah quickly looked down.

"No. It wasn't quite like that."

"No? Then why the eyes?"

She sat at her desk and looked at Leah with what seemed like genuine concern.

"I'd rather not talk about it."

Dillon didn't take her gaze off Leah.

"Suit yourself."

Leah tried to focus but could feel Dillon looking at her. She looked up.

"I crashed and burned last night. She wouldn't even let me try. I almost felt like giving up."

Dillon took a deep breath. She'd started this conversation. Did she really want to finish it?

"What do you mean? How could you crash and burn if she didn't let you try?"

Leah's eyes watered and she swallowed hard. Her voice cracked when she answered.

"She didn't like the way I sucked on her nipples. So I got frustrated and she accused me of throwing a hissy fit or something and got up and left."

Dillon went behind Leah and wrapped her arms around her. This is where Leah belonged. If only she could see that.

"I'm so sorry."

Leah wiped at a tear that had made its way down her cheek, then held Dillon's arms tight.

"It's just so damned hard. And how am I supposed to learn anything if someone walks out before I get my turn?"

"I'm sorry that happened."

Dillon was at a loss. She knew she should say something else, offer encouragement, but it was so hard for her.

"So are you going to give this app business a break?"

"I don't know. Part of me wants to."

"And why not listen to that part?"

"Because the main part of me really wants to learn so I can get Sueann back."

Dillon walked back to her seat.

"Are you sure Sueann is still single?"

"We've had this talk. I have to believe she is."

Dillon stood.

"Are you going to be okay? I should start making sure everything in the bar is ready to go."

Leah took a deep breath.

"I'll be fine. Thank you, though. You're the best."

Dillon bumped directly into Stephanie as she opened the office door. Stephanie looked from one to the other.

"Am I interrupting something?"

"Not a thing," Dillon said. "I was just going out to get things started and let Leah get the accounting done so she can get her errands run before lunch."

Dillon walked out of the office and closed the door behind her. Stephanie looked at her with an odd expression on her face.

"What?" Dillon said.

"I don't know. I mean, I get that it's none of my business, but she looks like she's been crying and you look like you've been put through the ringer as well. Should I be worried about my job? Is the bar going under?"

Dillon laughed.

"No. Nothing like that. The bar is fine, and if you keep up the excellent work you've been doing you'll never have to worry about a job."

"So, everything's okay? You're sure?"

"I'm sure. There's nothing for you to worry about. Now help me open the bar."

Stephanie sent her one more questioning look, but set about getting the bar ready.

The day passed fairly quickly. Dillon and Stephanie were quite a team behind the bar. Most of the time, Dillon hung back and watched Stephanie work her magic on the patrons. She got more tips even than Wy had gotten. Everyone loved her. Plus, she was so damned attractive. Dillon couldn't believe no one had swept her off her feet yet.

When the afternoon rolled around, Leah came out of the office. As usual, she was primed to take her turn behind the bar.

"No need," Dillon told her. "We've got this."

"But you've been behind the bar all day. Don't you want a break?"

"Sure. I'll sit down and eat a burger, but it's slow. If you want to check out early, you can."

"What's up? You want people to forget I own this place, too?" Leah laughed.

"Nothing like that. I just thought you might want to bug out early."

"Nope. I'm fine. And I think a turn behind the bar will be just what I need."

"Most excellent."

Dillon went into the kitchen and made herself a hamburger. She knew just how she liked it so she almost always made her own. She sat on the other side of the bar to eat. As she ate she watched Leah and Stephanie work behind the bar. Leah seemed strained, like she was forcing herself to be upbeat and friendly. But only to Stephanie. With everyone else, it seemed sincere.

She wondered anew what exactly Leah had against Stephanie. It seemed to be more than simply the fact that Dillon had hired her without consulting Leah. There seemed to be an animosity there that Dillon really didn't like. When she'd finished her lunch, she went back behind the bar.

"You sure you don't want me to take over now?"

"I'm sure," Leah said. "I'm having fun."

"Did you ever fill out the forms to take over the softball team?"

"No. I'm sorry."

"That's okay. I'll go do that right now. If you guys need me, I'll be in the office."

She pulled up the city softball league website and went about filling in the form. She was excited. She went back out to the bar.

"Hey, Stephanie?"

"Yeah?"

"Will you get the sizes for the women on the team? I'd like to order shirts for everyone."

"Sure. We have practice tonight."

"Excellent."

She went back to the office. She had nothing to do. Maybe she'd have a beer. She opened the door just as Leah was coming in.

"I have a date tonight," Leah said. Dillon noticed her voice shook slightly as she said it.

"You sure about doing this?"

"Sure I'm sure."

"You don't sound like it."

Leah sighed.

"I'm scared. I'll admit that. But I have to try."

"Okay. So what time will Princess Charming be here?"

"At six. Is that okay?"

"That's fine."

Then Stephanie was in the doorway.

"Hey, I could use some help."

Leah moved out of the way as Dillon went out to help with the happy hour rush. She didn't even give her a chance. She wanted to work. She needed to do something to keep her mind off yet another impending date. She hadn't even asked Leah who to be on the lookout for. She knew she'd have to, but she didn't want to. She wasn't ready yet.

The rush slowed down a bit.

"You think you can handle things from here on out?" Dillon said.

"Sure. Why? Are you leaving?"

"Nope. Just switching sides of the bar so I can have a beer."

"I'd say you've earned it."

Dillon sat and Stephanie placed a beer in front of her. She leaned on the bar, giving Dillon a lovely shot down her blouse to her ample boobs. She had nice tits, but Dillon shook her head. She was her employee. Besides, she wasn't on the market.

Leah came out of the office.

"Isn't there something you can be doing?" she said to Stephanie.

"Things have slowed down pretty much."

"Well, there are glasses to be washed. I don't like seeing you just lean."

"Sorry. I'll get on them."

"I'm going to go take a shower," Leah said to Dillon. "I'll be back around six."

"Sounds good. I'll be here."

As soon as she was out of the door, Stephanie walked over to Dillon.

"She really doesn't like me, does she?"

"Sure she does. She's just under a lot of stress. Don't worry. You're doing fine. She doesn't want to fire you or anything."

"But it bums me out that I can't win her over. I just want her not to hate me."

"She doesn't. Trust me."

"Okay. I'll try to believe you."

Dillon finished her beer and ordered another one.

"Am I going to be driving you home this evening?" Stephanie said.

"It's only two and I'll slow down. That first went down way too easily. I'm not even going to get buzzed. I'm just relaxing."

While she sat there, a patron came up and challenged her to a game of pool. She gladly accepted and won with ease. Several other women challenged her and she won all the games. She went back to the bar. It was five o'clock. Time for Stephanie to clock out, and she still had an hour before Leah got there.

"Are you hanging out until Leah gets back?"

"Yep. It's only another hour."

"Well, you've done a great job pacing yourself."

"Thanks. Can I buy you a glass of wine?"

"Sure." She sat next to Dillon. "So, why is Leah coming back?"

"She has another date."

"So, what's the story with all her dates? And why do you have to be here when she meets them?"

"Long story."

"In other words, it's none of my business."

Dillon smiled at her.

"It's just that it's Leah's story to tell. Not mine."

"And she'll never confide in me, so I just won't worry about it."

"There you go."

They sat sipping their drinks. Stephanie looked in the mirror behind the bar.

"She's here. And she looks very nice."

Dillon looked up. The sight took her breath away. Leah was gorgeous. She had on the blue dress she had started the whole app process in. Dillon had to tell herself to close her mouth. She wiped at it to make sure she hadn't been drooling.

"Yeah, she does," she said out loud.

Leah crossed the room to them.

"You look great," Stephanie said.

"Thanks. I'm a little nervous."

"No worries. You'll be great."

Leah looked to Dillon.

"Yeah. You look amazing. Whoever your date for the evening is is a lucky woman."

"Oh. That reminds me. I didn't show you her picture. Her name is Kayla."

Dillon took the phone. It was like looking at a younger version of Leah.

"She's cute. But do you think she's experienced enough?"

Leah shot a sidelong glance at Stephanie, and Dillon realized her mistake. She handed the phone back.

"Oh, my God. I think she's here," Leah said.

"You mean that beauty who just walked in?" Stephanie said.

"That looks to be her," Dillon said. "You sure you're ready?"

"Positive."

"She's coming this way," Stephanie said.

Soon Kayla was standing with them.

"Are you Leah?"

"Kayla?"

"Yes. You're beautiful."

"So are you."

Dillon wondered how they didn't realize how similar Kayla and Leah looked.

"This is my best friend, Dillon," Leah said. "And one of our bartenders, Stephanie."

"One of your bartenders?"

"Yes. We own the bar."

"How fun is that?"

"I know, right?" Leah said. "Would you like a drink?"

"No, thanks. I'll have wine with dinner. And speaking of dinner, we should get going."

"Sounds good," Leah said. And to Dillon, "See you tomorrow."

Left alone with her thoughts, Dillon contemplated staying at the bar and getting shitfaced. She figured she should be used to these sexual encounters of Leah by now, but each one seemed harder than the last.

"You okay?" Stephanie said.

Dillon had forgotten she was there.

"Huh? Yeah. I'm fine."

"Okay. Hey, you want to go grab dinner?"

"With you?"

"Sure." Stephanie laughed. "Why not? It'll be my treat."

"You don't have to buy."

"Does that mean you're considering it?"

"I don't know if it would be wise."

"Why not? Come on. I'm jonesin' for Mexican. And you look like you could use a margarita or two."

"I do, do I?" Dillon smiled. She hadn't realized her reaction to Leah and Kayla was written all over her.

"Yep. Now come on."

"Okay. Okay. I'm parked around back. You want to ride with me?"

"Sure."

They slipped out the delivery door and climbed into Dillon's truck.

"So what restaurant?"

Stephanie suggested one that was Dillon's favorite, so they drove there. It was slow, as was to be expected on a weeknight. They were seated in a back booth and conversation stopped while they perused their menus.

After they'd placed their orders, Stephanie looked at Dillon over the rim of her margarita.

"So, really, what's your story? I know you've told me before you're married to the bar, but really? Do you ever go out and have fun?"

"You know I'm still your boss, right?" Dillon smiled.

"I'm sorry. Sometimes I think of you as my friend, too."

"I'm just messin' with you. But what I said before still goes. I'm married to the bar. Happily so."

"But do you ever go out and have fun?"

"Where would you suggest I go? I own the only lesbian bar in town. I don't need everyone knowing my business."

"I guess that makes sense. I just hate to see a fine specimen such as yourself wasted."

"A fine specimen, huh?" Dillon laughed.

Stephanie blushed. It was the first time Dillon had seen her do that. She flirted plenty at the bar, and Dillon knew she was just flirting with her. But the blush confused her.

Their dinner arrived and Stephanie let the topic die. But after they were through, as they left the restaurant, she surprised Dillon again.

"Do we have to go back to the bar?"

"That's where your car is."

"I was thinking maybe we could go back to my place for a nightcap."

"A nightcap?" Dillon's stomach was in knots. Was that really all Stephanie wanted? Another drink? Or was she offering more? And if she did offer more, would she be strong enough to say no?

"Sure. Why not?"

"Yeah. You're right. Why the hell not?"

CHAPTER NINE

Dillon followed Stephanie's directions and arrived at a cute little house on the east side of town.

"Is this yours or do you rent?" Dillon said when she parked in the driveway.

"I rent. But I've made it my own."

"Very good. I can't wait to see what it looks like on the inside." Though she could, in fact, wait. She was a nervous wreck and was trying to figure out how to get out of this situation. She chided herself that she was a grown-up and that she was free to do whatever she wanted.

"Then let's go in and see."

Dillon climbed out of the truck then went around to open Stephanie's door. Stephanie allowed herself to be helped out. She held on to Dillon's hand just a second too long. Dillon almost pulled away, but it struck something inside her. Something deep inside her responded to the touch in a way she hadn't responded to any woman but Leah in far too long. Was this a good thing? Or not?

Stephanie opened the door and stood aside to let Dillon in. Dillon took in the country style of decorations all over.

"I never took you for a country gal," Dillon said.

"I grew up on a farm. I guess I still like the décor. Have a seat on the couch. I'll go get you a beer."

Dillon sat. She was getting a beer. So, it was all about a nightcap after all. She took a deep breath and relaxed. Stephanie was back in no time with a beer for Dillon and a glass of wine for herself. There was something different about her. Dillon couldn't put her finger on it, but she seemed somehow more attractive, more seductive.

"Are you okay, Dillon?"

"Huh? Yeah. I'm fine."

Dillon shifted in her seat. Parts below her waist had come alive, and she tried to get comfortable and take pressure off them.

"So, I have something to ask you," Stephanie said.

Dillon took a long pull off her beer, but it didn't help with the heat that had filled the room.

"Go for it."

"Would you like to stay the night?" Stephanie said.

"What? Here?"

Stephanie laughed and placed her warm hand on Dillon's thigh.

"Yes. Here. With me."

"I don't know, Stephanie."

"What's not to know?" She leaned in closer so her face was only inches from Dillon's. Dillon could barely breathe. The room seemed devoid of oxygen.

"Stephanie, I'm your boss."

"I know that. And you will be tomorrow. But for tonight, won't you just be my lover?"

She moved closer yet. Dillon felt frozen in place. Her heart thudded. She knew she should get up and drive home, but she couldn't. Why couldn't she? Because, damn it, she wanted Stephanie. She wanted to spend the night with a beautiful woman. And Stephanie was offering.

"Will things be awkward at work tomorrow?"

"No. I promise."

"Okay then."

"Really?" Stephanie said.

"Really."

Dillon leaned in and brushed Stephanie's lips. The light touch sent shockwaves shooting through her body. It was nice, but Dillon wanted, no needed, more. She kissed her again, harder this time, and Stephanie returned her kiss with equal fervor. Dillon was craving the feel of Stephanie under her and eased her back on the couch. She climbed on top of her and ground her pelvis into her. She was so wet and so swollen and so ready to take Stephanie.

Stephanie wrapped her legs around Dillon and pulled her to her. Their tongues danced frantically while their bodies writhed and thrust against each other. Dillon reached under Stephanie's shirt and closed her hand on her full breast held captive by a lacy bra. Dillon finally came up for air.

"I need you, Stephanie. I need you naked. I need to see you, taste you, take you. Please. Where's your bedroom?"

Stephanie let Dillon help her to her feet. She led them down the hall to a small bedroom. Dillon had barely stepped inside when she pulled Stephanie's shirt over her head. Next came her bra. She stood there staring at Stephanie's naked breasts until she could stand it no longer. She bent and took one with both hands.

"My God, you're beautiful," she whispered.

She kneaded the mounds for a long time before she teased her nipples with her fingers. She twisted and pulled on them, then bent to take them both in her mouth at once. Damn, Stephanie was sexy as hell.

She pulled down Stephanie's skirt and braced her while she stepped out of it. Last to come off were her panties, which Dillon pressed to her nose.

"You smell divine," she said.

Stephanie climbed on the bed and propped herself up on an elbow and watched as Dillon quickly shed her own clothes.

"Damn, your body is as fine as I'd imagined," Stephanie said. "You're a piece of work. Get up here. Now."

Dillon joined Stephanie on the bed and kissed her again. This time, while their tongues played over each other, Dillon slid her hand down Stephanie's body to her tight center. She easily slid two fingers in. She wanted to add more, to go deeper, to climb inside with her whole body to enjoy that wet silkiness. But she could tell two fingers was all Stephanie could take. She was oh-so tight. She moved her fingers in and out, fucking her in the wanton way she seemed to want. While she thrust, Stephanie reached her own hand between her legs and rubbed her clit. Dillon felt the spasms start inside just before Stephanie called her name.

Dillon settled between Stephanie's legs and lapped up the remnants of her orgasm. She tasted wonderful just as Dillon had known she would. She was sweet and musky and Dillon couldn't get enough.

She licked all over before settling in at Stephanie's clit. It was slick and delicious, and in no time, Stephanie was crying out again. Dillon climbed up next to Stephanie, who quickly slid between her legs. She kissed down one inner thigh and up the other. Dillon could feel her clit swelling and worried it might burst. But Stephanie was in no hurry. She lay there between Dillon's legs, not moving.

"You're beautiful," she said. "Just gorgeous."

"Thank you." She wanted to scream for Stephanie to take her already, but she didn't. She gritted her teeth and waited for the attention she so desperately needed. Finally, Stephanie's tongue was exploring all the tender spots between her legs. She sucked her lips and licked her deep inside. She kissed her way to Dillon's clit which was so ready it took only moments for Dillon to feel her whole body tense and release and float slowly back to earth.

Stephanie moved into Dillon's arms.

"That was something else," Dillon said.

"Yeah, it was. You sure know what you're doing. But I knew you would."

Dillon propped herself up and looked into Stephanie's glistening eyes.

"You did, huh? And how long have you been pondering that?"

"Since before I started working for you," Stephanie said matter-of-factly.

"No shit?"

"No shit. You're hotter than hot, Dillon. Surely you know that the women in the bar, well, at least the femmes in the bar, all lust after you."

"I had no idea."

"Bullshit. You've got to be kidding me."

"I own that place. It's my baby. It's my job. I just want everyone to have fun. It never occurred to me anyone fantasized about me."

"Well, I certainly have. And we just had fun, right? So, the bar can lead to fun."

"Yes. I suppose it can. I guess I should get going now."

"What's the hurry? If you go now, you'll have to drive me to the bar to get my car and then home. Why not just stay here?"

Dillon looked at the gorgeous body of Stephanie's lying next to her and decided it wouldn't hurt to stay. Who knew? It might even lead to more play time later.

❖

Leah had enjoyed her dinner with Kayla and was relaxed and ready to try her hand at pleasing her. Everything about Kayla made her comfortable. She felt completely at ease with her. She only hoped that would lead to fun in bed. They arrived back at her house.

"Would you like another glass of wine?" Leah said.

"Sure. That would be great."

"Have a seat on the couch. I'll bring it out."

Leah walked out to the couch to find Kayla sitting there in just her bra and panties. She stopped halfway to the couch.

"Oh my," she said.

"I thought I'd get comfortable. It's okay, isn't it? I mean, isn't the end result of tonight going to be sex? I didn't misunderstand, did I?"

Leah fought to find her voice. The vision in front of her had left her speechless.

"No. You're right. It's just… I mean… well… I just didn't expect to see you like this when I walked back into the room. But it's fine. I mean, it's better than fine. It's quite nice, actually."

"Won't you join me? I wouldn't mind seeing you in your underwear."

"Well, the truth is, I don't wear underwear. At least not on the bottom."

"Even better. Come on, Leah. Strip down for me. We'll sip our wine like this."

Leah stood still holding the wine. She knew her hesitation was unreasonable. Kayla would see her naked eventually anyway. She handed a glass of wine to Kayla and set hers on the table. She took off her dress and stood self-consciously in front of Kayla wearing nothing but her blue satin bra.

"Damn. You're gorgeous," Kayla said. "I mean like, wow, kind of gorgeous."

Leah felt the blush start at her chest and work its way up.

"Thank you. So are you."

Kayla patted the spot next to her on the couch.

"Come here. Sit."

Leah sat next to Kayla and could feel the heat radiating off of her. She was so damned sexy. Leah was sure they would have fun later. Or even sooner at the rate they were going.

Kayla placed her hand on Leah's thigh while they drank their wine. Occasionally, she would slide it up a little, almost to Leah's throbbing center, but then she'd move it again.

"I can't believe a woman like you doesn't know how to please a woman," Kayla said.

Leah shrugged. She'd had this conversation so many times.

"I just can't. I try, but I always screw something up."

"I bet you're just used to being pleased, right? I mean, who could be in a room with you and not want to take you places you've never been before?"

"That's very sweet of you. I don't know that it's true, but thank you."

"So who told you you were lousy in bed? I mean, what prompted you to post your profile on Girl World?"

"My ex. She broke up with me after five years. The main reason she gave was that I couldn't satisfy her in bed."

"Ouch. She sounds like a bitch," Kayla said.

"Not really. I can't say I blame her. I'm sure she'll come back to me after I learn what I'm doing."

"Seriously? After she said that to you, you'd still take her back?"

"Of course. I love her."

Kayla just shook her head.

"If you say so. I'd say good riddance."

Leah didn't like the way the conversation was going. She didn't like anyone bad-mouthing Sueann. Especially someone who likely didn't know her and never would.

"I think we should talk about something else. This is kind of killing the mood."

Kayla moved closer to Leah on the couch. She nuzzled her neck.

"Oh no, baby," she said. "I don't want anything to ruin the mood. You're here, half naked with a woman who wants you desperately. That should definitely help your mood."

The sensations Kayla was causing washed over her body. Both nipples and her clit stood at attention. She was ready.

"Did you want to finish your wine?" Leah said.

"Yep. I want to draw this out." She placed her hand high up on Leah's thigh. "Though I can feel from here how ready you are. I bet you're delicious, too. Are you?"

"I can't say I've ever tasted myself."

"Even on a lover's lips? Mm. I'm sure you taste marvelous."

Her low voice, barely over a whisper, sent chills over Leah's body. With a shaky hand, she picked up her wine glass and took a sip. She wanted to gulp it down, to set her glass on the table, stand up, and take Kayla to her bedroom. *Be patient.* It was almost time.

"What are you thinking?" Kayla said.

"Just how I want to take you to my room right now."

"All in due time, my dear. The night is still young. Now, I'm not totally comfortable. Would you mind if I take off my bra?"

Would she mind? She'd like nothing better. But she didn't want to appear too eager.

"That would be nice," she said.

She watched Kayla remove her lacy bra. Her pert breasts looked to be about a handful, but that was plenty for Leah. She knew she would enjoy them.

"That's better," Kayla said.

Leah leaned in and kissed her then, needing to taste her lips. They were soft and tasted of wine. It was a heady combination.

"That was nice," Kayla said. "May I have another?"

Leah was happy to oblige. This time Kayla opened her mouth, and soon their tongues were tangoing. Leah was careful about how much she put in Kayla's mouth which Kayla seemed to appreciate.

"Damn," she said when the kiss ended. "You sure know how to kiss."

"So do you," Leah said. She was short of breath and itching for more.

They finally finished their wine and Leah stood. Kayla was still sitting and her face was right where Leah's legs met. Kayla grabbed Leah's ass and pulled her to her. She slid her tongue between her legs and ran it over her clit. It felt so good that Leah almost fell over, but Kayla was holding on tight.

"Spread your legs," she said.

Leah spread them as wide as she could and still keep her balance.

Kayla dropped to her knees and licked every inch between Leah's legs. Leah felt her muscles tighten. Her stomach was a bundle of knots. She knew she was going to come.

"I'm going to fall."

"I've got you. Come for me, Leah."

Kayla went back to what she was doing and Leah lost all thought as wave after wave of orgasms rolled over her. Kayla finally stood and kissed her.

"See? You do taste amazing."

But Leah was too lightheaded to acknowledge. She was still afraid she would fall even though Kayla had her arms around her and was holding her tight. When Leah finally came out of her haze, she smiled at Kayla.

"That was wonderful. But now it's my turn, and I'm going to have to insist we go to bed."

"Sure."

In the bedroom, they each took off the remainder of their clothes and lay together, skin on skin. Kayla's skin was so soft, Leah felt herself becoming aroused all over again just touching it. She gently suckled her nipples, and Kayla must have enjoyed it as she tangled her fingers in her hair to hold her there.

"Oh yes. Oh dear God, that feels good," she said.

Leah smiled as she kissed down her soft belly and spread her legs so she could climb between. She inhaled deeply at the musky scent that was Kayla.

"You smell delicious," she said.

"I hope you'll think I taste that way, too."

"I'm sure I will."

Kayla was glistening down there from one end to the other, and Leah finally decided it was time to try to please her. She lowered her head and made her cursive alphabet like Donna had taught her.

"That feels amazing," Kayla said.

Leah slipped two fingers inside. She moved them in and out and all around.

"More. Give me more."

She slid another finger in and continued what she was doing. While she did that, she licked her way to Leah's clit. It was small, but hard, and Leah licked and sucked at it until Kayla cried out. Leah stopped what she was doing, shocked. She lifted her head and looked up at Kayla.

"Did I really do it? Did you come?"

"Oh, baby. You'd better believe it. You were fantastic. Don't let anyone tell you you don't know what you're doing again. You're a natural."

Leah was all smiles as she made her way up to kiss Kayla.

"I can't believe it. I really can't believe I did that."

"Really? Well, believe it, sister. You got me off big time."

They lay together in silence for a few minutes.

"Well, I guess I'd better get going," Kayla said.

Leah contemplated for a minute the idea of inviting her to stay the night. But no, it was a one-night deal.

"Yeah. I suppose it's that time."

"I could stay, if you wanted me to."

"I don't think that would be a good idea."

"Okay. I'll get my things then."

Once Kayla was gone, Leah lay in bed smiling so wide her face hurt. She couldn't have wiped it off if she tried. She couldn't wait to tell Dillon about it in the morning.

CHAPTER TEN

When Dillon pulled into work the next morning, she saw that Leah was already there. Shit. Dillon was also dropping Stephanie off to pick up her car. Leah knew Stephanie's car, and since it was the only one in the parking lot, she would soon put two and two together. Shit.

"Can I come in and get some coffee?" Stephanie said.

"You don't want to go home and change?"

"Yeah. I suppose I should."

"Look. I'd kind of like to keep last night just between the two of us," Dillon said.

"I can be discreet."

"Thank you."

"What will you tell Leah?"

"That you called me and asked for a ride to get your car. She doesn't need to know we left together last night."

"Sounds good. Okay. Well, thanks for the lift. And thanks for last night. If you ever want to do it again, just let me know, okay?"

"Yes, ma'am."

She watched Stephanie get out of her truck and climb in her car. When she'd backed out, Dillon went around to the back and parked her truck in her usual spot. She braced herself for a barrage of questions as she let herself into the office.

"Good morning," she said.

"And a lovely good morning to you."

Dillon was confused. Where were the questions? Was Leah being sarcastic? She normally didn't beat around the bush. What was up with her?

"You seem like you're in a good mood."

"I am. I got Kayla off last night and she told me I'm a natural. A natural, Dillon. How about that? I knew what I was doing and I pleased her in the most wonderful of ways."

Dillon's stomach turned over. So this was why she hadn't noticed Dillon dropping Stephanie off. She supposed she should have been relieved, but all she could think about was Leah making love to her doppelgänger. It did nothing to settle her. Why did Leah feel the need to share everything with her?

"Aren't you going to say anything?" Leah looked at her expectantly. "Like congratulate me or something?"

"Sure. I think it's great. Good job. So are you through searching for women now?"

"I don't know. I think I want to find Sueann and try it out on her first."

"Listen, Leah, I really want you to think long and hard before you do that. She broke your heart into a million tiny pieces. Do you really want to give her the power to do that again?"

"But she won't. I'll make her feel amazing things and she'll take me back. Don't you get it?" Leah said.

"And what if she's moved on?"

"I doubt she has. She loved me. It would take her a while to go on to someone else."

Dillon was at a loss. What could she say to Leah to make her realize Sueann was a bitch and she was setting herself up for more heartbreak?

"Well, I'll leave you to the accounting," Dillon said. "I'll start setting up the bar."

"By the way, it appears I'm not the only one who got lucky last night," Leah said.

Dillon froze. Her stomach balled into a cold fist.

"What do you mean?" she said.

"I saw Stephanie's car in the lot. Didn't you see it? Maybe not. She might have picked it up already. At any rate, she didn't take herself home last night."

"Maybe she got too drunk to drive."

"I doubt it. I think she finally gave in to someone. She seems like she's so warm and caring behind the bar, but you never see her leave with anyone. It's like she's an ice princess."

"Am I an ice princess, too, then?" Dillon said.

"No, handsome. You're an ice prince. With too many secrets to keep. But that's okay. I love you anyway."

"Gee, thanks."

Dillon went out to set up the bar. She wished Leah would say she loved her like she meant it. She was almost ready to open when Stephanie came in.

"Sorry I'm a little late."

Dillon checked the clock.

"Only five minutes. I wouldn't worry about it."

"Hey now," Stephanie said quietly. "No favors because I slept with the boss."

Dillon forced a smile on her face. She again wondered at the wisdom in it all. But damn, it had been fun and had felt so good. And now Stephanie was standing so near her, with her hair still damp from her shower. She smelled clean and fresh and devourable. Dillon told her libido to calm down. She had a whole day of work ahead. And she vowed she wasn't going to go home with Stephanie again. It was too dangerous and too easy. And she wasn't Leah and never would be.

Stephanie finished the opening process and Dillon went into the office to work on social media before the lunch rush started. She looked over at Leah who looked up at her with a big smile on her face.

"Isn't it a beautiful day?"

"If you say so."

"I do. You know. You should get laid once in a while. It might help your mood."

"My mood is just fine," Dillon said. "Now I'm going to work on our sites while you go do your thing."

"I'm off now. I'll be back by eleven."

"Sounds good."

Dillon was posting their upcoming specials when there was a knock on the office door.

"Come in."

Stephanie walked in.

"Hey," she said.

"Hey."

"Are we okay?"

"Yeah. We're fine."

"You sure?"

"Of course."

"I enjoyed last night," Stephanie said.

"So did I."

"I wouldn't mind a repeat."

"Stephanie, I have to be honest. I'm not looking for a relationship. I'm not going to get emotionally involved with you."

"But we can still have fun, right?"

"Maybe. We'll see."

"Okay. I'd better get back behind the bar."

Dillon sank low in her seat. She knew she wanted Stephanie again. There was no denying it. But would it be fair to either of them to do it again?

Leah was back before lunch, as promised. She sat at the bar and watched Dillon and Stephanie work through the rush. They worked so well together, but that day something seemed different. She couldn't put her finger on it, but it seemed there was something between them. She didn't like it. She didn't know what her problem with Stephanie was. She'd always enjoyed her as a patron, but she really didn't like her as a bartender. She was good at it. And the patrons loved her, but she didn't. But she wasn't sure why.

The lunch rush was over and it was the lull before happy hour. She went behind the bar, still flying high from the night before. It was slow and she leaned on the bar and daydreamed about how good Kayla had tasted and how right it had felt pleasing her.

"You with us?" Stephanie finally said.

"Hmm? Yeah. Sorry. Just lost in thought."

"How did your date go last night?"

Leah's first thought was to tell her it was none of her business. But she was only making conversation and there was no reason to be a bitch.

"It was great. How was yours?"

"Mine?" Stephanie blushed.

"Yeah. I noticed your car was still here this morning."

"I just had a little too much to drink. So I got a ride home from someone. I'm not taking any chances, you know?"

"I don't blame you there."

"No. Well, I'm glad you had a good time. She seemed really nice."

"She was."

"Are you going to see her again?"

"I don't know, to be honest."

"Oh," Stephanie said.

"It's kind of complicated."

"Isn't it always?"

The place started to fill up again, and Dillon joined them behind the bar. Happy hour kept them steadily working until five o'clock.

"What are everybody's plans for tonight?" Stephanie said.

"I have no idea," Leah said.

"Actually," Dillon said, "I was hoping Leah and I could go out for dinner and discuss business."

"Sounds like a blast," Stephanie said.

"I think it sounds good. We've got the pool tournament coming up and other events we need to make sure we're ready for."

The bar was under control with two evening bartenders working.

"Shall we go now then?" Dillon said.

"Sounds good."

"I'll see you both tomorrow," Stephanie said and they all left the bar.

"I bet if I ask, you'll take Mexican, right?" Dillon said.

"Of course." Leah smiled. "I'll meet you there."

They were seated at a booth by the front of the restaurant. Neither needed a menu, as they'd been there so many times they knew exactly what they wanted. They were discussing upcoming events when Dillon got a strange look on her face. Leah turned to see what she was looking at. There was Sueann holding hands with another woman while they waited for a table.

Leah was out of the booth before she really thought about it.

"Sueann," she said. "How are you?"

"Leah," she said. "I'm fine. How are you?"

"I'm great."

Leah looked to the woman Sueann was with.

"Oh, Leah, this is my girlfriend, Nadia."

The words hit Leah like a punch in the gut. A girlfriend? So soon?

"Nice to meet you." She forced herself to say.

Nadia extended her hand. Leah took it and tried to think of something more to say.

"It's wonderful to meet you, too," Nadia said. "I've heard so much about you."

Did you hear I was lousy in bed? Are you wonderful in bed? The thoughts that raced through Leah's minds weren't healthy.

"Well, it looks like our dinner has been served, so I should go," she said.

"It was great seeing you," Sueann said.

"Yeah. You, too."

She made her way back to her table and sat down, fighting tears.

"You going to be okay?" Dillon said.

"No. She has a new girlfriend. How can that be?"

A tear slid down her cheek. She wiped it away.

Dillon reached out and took her hand.

"It'll be okay," she said. "You'll move on."

"But I don't want to move on."

"You have to. She has and now it's time for you to. Now eat your dinner. We can go back to the bar and drink our sorrows away."

"I'm not hungry."

"You should eat something."

"I want a margarita."

"Okay. We'll order you one. But please eat something."

Leah didn't know how she could with the rock in her stomach, but she took a bite and it didn't taste as much like cardboard as she'd expected. She took another and another and soon, half her meal was gone. She sat back in the booth.

"I can't eat another bite. But I want another margarita."

"What do you say we go to The Kitty? We can drink there."

"I can't cry there."

"You really want to cry here? Let's go back to my place. I'll fix you a drink or two."

"Or ten," Leah said.

Dillon laughed.

"Or ten."

"It's not funny," Leah said.

"No, the situation is not. But the idea of you drinking ten margaritas is."

"I just can't believe this is happening."

"Come on. Let's go."

Leah followed Dillon to her house just a few blocks from her own. It was a nice ranch style home decorated in leathers and dark woods. It was very masculine and suited Dillon. It was quite the opposite of her own airy style.

She sat on the leather couch and kicked her shoes off. She tucked her feet under her while she waited for Dillon to bring her a drink. Leah knew she had to be careful. Much more to drink and she'd be in danger of not driving. And then where would that leave her? Taking a cab home? She didn't think Dillon should drive after much more either.

Dillon was back and sat next to her on the couch. Leah set her drink down and buried her face in Dillon's shoulder and cried. Dillon placed an arm around Leah and held her tight. This wasn't how she wanted to be holding her, but she knew Leah needed a friend right then and not a lover. It broke Dillon's heart to see how hurt Leah was. She wished she'd been able to keep a neutral face when she'd seen Sueann, but she hadn't and she couldn't change the past.

Leah finally stopped crying and sat up. Dillon got her a box of tissues.

"Thanks," Leah said.

"I really am sorry, kiddo."

"I know. Me, too. I need to go splash my face."

"You know where the bathroom is."

When Leah was in the bathroom, Dillon's phone buzzed. She checked the text. It was from Stephanie.

Feel like coming over tonight? It said.

Can't. Sorry.

K. Sorry to bother you.

No bother. She thought about it, then typed. *Appreciate the invitation.*

There. She'd said it. Yes. She did appreciate it. But her first concern was Leah and making sure she was okay.

Leah came back and sat on the couch. She sipped her margarita.

"This is really good."

"I should know a little something about mixing drinks," Dillon said.

Leah smiled. Her beauty shone through even with her swollen, red-framed eyes. Damn, she took Dillon's breath away.

She took a long pull of her beer. She'd switched back to beer to keep her senses somewhat sharp. She didn't want to get drunk and do anything stupid.

Leah finished her drink and Dillon mixed her another one.

"You want to listen to music or anything?" Dillon said.

"No. I want to sit here with you and wallow in my self-pity."

"How long do you plan to do that?"

"As long as I need to."

Great, Dillon thought. She'd have to be the strong, dependable friend for a while now. Would she be able to make a move? Doubtful. She was in the friend zone now and that's likely where she'd stay.

"So, about that app…" Dillon said.

"Yeah. I'll get back to it. At least there are some women out there who appreciate me."

"But you've learned all you need to know, right?"

"I've learned a lot, but what good will it do me if I never practice it?"

"Are you going to change your profile?"

"No," Leah said.

"Why not?"

"Why should I? I still need to learn. So I've gotten two women off. Big deal. There's a lot more women that I haven't. So I'll keep my profile just how it is."

Dillon noticed a slight slur to Leah's words. She knew Leah was too drunk to drive. She wondered if she was okay behind a wheel. Doubtful. A DUI could affect the bar, so she didn't want to take any chances.

"I think I'm drunk," Leah said.

"Yeah? Nothing wrong with that."

"No? Okay. Can I have another then?"

"Sure."

Dillon mixed another drink. While she was in the kitchen, she checked her texts. There was another from Stephanie that she hadn't heard come in.

Really? You appreciate it?

Really. I do. Just busy right now.

Thanks.

For?

Making me feel good.

Dillon didn't respond. She finished mixing Leah's drink and took it out to her. She found Leah asleep on the couch. She set the drink down and carefully lifted Leah and carried her back to her bedroom. She gently placed her on the bed.

Leah opened her eyes briefly.

"Shhh," Dillon said. "Just go to sleep."

Dillon grabbed a blanket and a pillow and lay on the couch. She closed her eyes, but sleep didn't come. Her thoughts were jumbled between Leah and Stephanie. What was she doing? With either?

CHAPTER ELEVEN

Dillon woke the next morning to the sound of her shower. It took her a moment to clear the cobwebs enough to remember Leah had spent the night. She lay back on the couch and listened to the sound. She closed her eyes and imagined a naked Leah with water droplets running down her perfect body. She sat bolt upright. Those were not healthy thoughts. She got up and made coffee.

Leah came into the kitchen wearing a towel.

"Good morning," Dillon said.

"Is it?"

She moved into Dillon's arms and Dillon held her, trying not to think about how soft and smooth her skin was. That wasn't where her brain should be at that moment.

"Oh, Dillon. What am I going to do?"

"Move on. She has and you should."

"I was thinking in the shower."

"Yeah? What did you come up with?"

"I think I might see if Kayla wants to get together again. She was fun. And she could keep my mind off Sueann. At least for a couple of hours."

"I thought your deal with these women was for one night only."

Dillon couldn't stand the thought of Leah seeing someone else. Not now. She'd only split up with Sueann six or so months ago. How could she think of getting into a serious relationship now?

"I don't plan on making this long-term. Just something to do so I don't wallow away in self-pity another night."

"Well, I don't mind being your shoulder if you need another one tonight," Dillon said.

"Thanks. And you're great. But you can't offer me what they do, you know?"

No, Dillon wanted to scream. I don't know, because I can offer you that and so much more. But she kept her thoughts to herself.

"Got it," was all she said.

"I'd better get dressed and head home to change for work," Leah said.

"Yeah and I'd better get a move on here."

"Okay. I'll see you in an hour or so."

"Sounds good."

"And, Dillon?"

"Yeah?"

"Thanks for last night."

"No problem."

Dillon sat for a moment in her quiet house after Leah left. She felt like her heart was breaking, too. Why was Leah not attracted to her? Stephanie clearly was. And according to her, lots of women were, so why not Leah? What would she have to do to win her over?

She showered and drove to work. Leah wasn't there yet, and Dillon sat in the office contemplating what to do with Stephanie. She was so much fun in bed. And she took her mind off Leah for a few hours, but Dillon wasn't emotionally attracted to her. If she explained that to Stephanie, would it hurt her feelings? Could they just sleep together?

Stephanie showed up and interrupted her thoughts. Her shirt was so tight, Dillon was worried she would pop out of it. She had such great tits. Dillon had to give her credit for that. She just looked overly hot. Or maybe Dillon was just overly horny.

"Good morning," Stephanie said.

"Well, hello. You're here early."

"I was hoping to get here before Leah."

"Yeah? Why? What's up?"

Just then the bells on the front door rang and Stephanie looked out into the bar.

"Never mind. She's here."

She walked back to the bar.

Dillon got up from her spot behind the desk.

"Good morning, Leah," she said.

"Good morning. I'll be working the numbers. Stephanie, why are you here so early?"

"I couldn't sleep. I figured I could maybe start helping with the cleaning and stuff before we open once in a while."

"I'd love that," Dillon said.

"We'll see," Leah said then disappeared in the office.

Dillon rolled her eyes.

"See?" Stephanie practically hissed. "She really doesn't like me."

"I think she just wants to be sure we're staying under budget. She's the number cruncher, you know."

"Yeah. I know."

"So, what did you want to talk to me about?"

"Last night."

"What about it?" Dillon said.

"I'm really sorry I bugged you."

"You didn't. Not at all."

"Well, I feel like I did. What with you being busy and all."

"I was helping a friend through a rough patch. That's all, so I couldn't text much." She lowered her voice. "Or come over."

"So you're not upset?"

"No. Like I said. I appreciated the offer. Honest. I wish I could have taken you up on it."

"No lie?"

"No lie," Dillon said. "Now, come on. Let's get cleaning. We need to open soon."

They got the bar opened and Stephanie was flirting with Martha and some of the other old timers when Leah came out to announce she was going to the bank and to run errands. Dillon was standing back watching Stephanie. She took in her long legs and shapely ass, and suddenly, she knew what she wanted to be doing that night. Or rather, who she wanted to be doing. Stephanie was just too fun not to enjoy again.

Dillon leaned on the counter next to her and started visiting with the regulars.

"Why don't you two get together?" Martha said. "You're both good-looking and single. Dillon, you're butch and she's femme. You'd be perfect together."

Dillon looked away and coughed to cover up anything that might show on her face. She looked over at Stephanie who was blushing. Damn.

"Aha, at least the lady's thought about it," Martha said. "Now it's time for you to quit being so stubborn and ask her out, Dillon."

"I'm her boss. That would be awkward."

"Nonsense. Stranger things have happened."

"I have work to do in my office. Feel free to discuss my dating life without me."

She went into the office and powered up her laptop. She still had some advertising to do and some last-minute details to work out for the pool tournament, since she and Leah hadn't discussed anything about it the previous night.

She was working away when there was a knock on the door.

"Come in."

Stephanie popped her head in.

"Sorry about all that. It was all in fun."

"No worries. I don't mind. Though your blushing doesn't help."

"Sorry about that, too."

"Seriously. I don't mind. I would only mind if you actually told someone about that night and I trust that you won't."

"My lips are sealed."

She left the office and Dillon wondered when they'd get together again. She'd like to that night, but should she make the first move? Or leave that up to Stephanie? She shook her head. Sleeping with an employee was complicated. And probably not smart. But oh-so-much fun.

Leah was back from running errands. She dropped the meats for lunch in the kitchen then went into the office. She collapsed onto her chair.

"What's up?" Dillon said.

"You'll never believe who I saw at the butcher shop. At *our* butcher shop. The one we've used for five years now."

"I have no idea. Who?"

"Fucking Sueann."

"Really?"

"Yes. She apparently was buying steaks or something. I don't know."

"Are you okay?"

"No. Not even close. I'm pissed. She had to know I'd be there. She lived with me for five years. She knew my daily routine as well as you do."

"So what did she say? Anything?"

"Yes. She apologized for running into me the night before. She'd been meaning to let me know she'd met someone. She didn't mean for it to happen in a public place. Oh, my God. She's such a bitch."

She looked at Dillon for some response, but Dillon's face was neutral. Almost too neutral.

"But it's okay." She went on. "I'm moving on, too. I have a date with Kayla tonight. So there. Take that, Sueann."

"So do you think Kayla is going to be a regular thing for you? I mean do you like her?"

"I like her a lot, but no, not like that. I mean, I could never settle down with her. She'll just be someone to pass the time with tonight. Hopefully soon I'll get some other offers. I may update my profile to say I've learned a little but need practice. How does that sound?"

"You know how I feel about that app, kiddo. So I don't know if I'm the person to be asking."

"But you're my best friend. Who else can I ask?"

"Okay. I suppose it sounds better and you might get more people if they think you've got more experience now."

"Thanks. That's what I thought, too. I'll do that in just a minute."

"I need to get out to help Stephanie now. I'll see you in a few."

Leah updated her profile as soon as Dillon was out of the office. She thought it sounded better and made her look a little less desperate. Though she was careful to say she was still inexperienced and needed practice. She finished with the accounting program just as the lunch rush ended. She walked out to the bar to take over for Dillon.

She saw Dillon and Stephanie whispering.

"Am I interrupting something?" she said.

"Not at all," Dillon said. "We're just shooting the shit."

"Well, you can go relax for a while. I'm here now."

Why did Dillon and Stephanie bother her so much? She figured it must be because Dillon was her best friend and she didn't like sharing her with Stephanie. Stephanie was an employee, not a friend, but sometimes she thought Dillon forgot that.

Dillon made herself a burger and sat at the bar with a beer. Leah stood there talking to her, making sure Stephanie couldn't get to her. Stephanie busied herself with bussing tables and washing dishes. Leah was actually enjoying herself when she looked up to see Kayla walk in.

"What are you doing here so early?" Leah said.

"I just wanted to see you. Is that okay? Plus, I've heard you guys serve really good burgers and I'm starving."

"Don't you have to work?"

"I took the afternoon off. I thought maybe you could sneak out early, too."

"Well, grab a burger and then we'll talk about leaving."

Kayla ordered then sat next to Dillon.

"Hi, Dillon."

"Hi, Kayla. How are you?"

"Famished. And you?" She laughed.

"I just finished a burger, so I'm great. And I'm on my break from work. So it's all good right now."

"Good for you. Do you think it'll be okay if Leah cuts out early?"

"I own this place, too, you know," Leah said. "And I'm perfectly capable of taking an afternoon off as long as the bar doesn't need me."

"And I don't think the bar will need you," Dillon said.

"Me, either."

"Great," Kayla said. "That's awesome."

Kayla ate her burger and it was time for Dillon to relieve Leah anyway. Leah said good-bye and left with Kayla.

"You want me to follow you to your place again?" Kayla said.

"Yes. I'd like that."

"Okay. Lead the way."

Leah pulled into her driveway and Kayla parked by the curb. They got out and went inside.

"I was wondering," Kayla said. "How would you feel about a shower? I mean, since we both had to work part days. It might feel good."

A shower with Kayla? Leah could think of worse ways to spend her afternoon.

"I think I'd like that."

"Great."

Leah took her soft, smooth hand and led her down the hall, through her bedroom, to the master bath. She had a double-headed shower, perfect for two people. But she was sure they would probably share one shower head.

The idea of slipping and sliding against a sudsy Kayla made her pulse race. They stripped down and climbed into the shower. Kayla lathered Leah up first. She ran her hands all over her body, bringing one to a stop when she reached between Leah's legs. She slipped inside and Leah fought to stay on her feet as Kayla slid her hand from her middle and rubbed her clit. Leah screamed at the intensity of the orgasm that rocked her body.

She knew it was her turn. Her heart slowed to almost normal and she dropped to a knee and buried her face between Kayla's legs. She added her fingers while she licked her clit. Soon she felt Kayla's fingernails digging into her shoulders as she reached her own climax.

They rinsed and dried and walked hand in hand to the bedroom.

"Climb up," Kayla said. "And spread your arms and legs wide for me."

Leah did as she was asked. She kind of liked being spread-eagle for Kayla. She liked the idea that she could see her so easily. What she didn't like was when Kayla reached into her bags and pulled out some scarves.

"Wait a minute," Leah said.

"Sh. It's okay. I'm not going to hurt you. It'll be fun. Trust me."

Leah didn't move, but certainly didn't calm down. She was nervous. She could almost feel her clit shrink. Kayla must have noticed while she was tying her ankles to her bed.

"You're nervous. Don't be. This is just another way to have fun. And don't worry, you'll get your turn when I'm through with you."

When Leah was secured, Kayla got up on the bed with her. She skimmed her hand all over her body.

"You're beautiful," she said. "Just beautiful."

Leah felt her body respond to Kayla's touch. She might have been uncomfortable, but now she didn't care. She just wanted Kayla to touch her more, to please her, to get her off. Kayla climbed off the bed and reached into her bag again, but whatever she got out of it, she hid from Leah.

"What's that?" Leah said.

"You'll find out soon enough."

Kayla ran her hand down between Leah's legs.

"That's a good girl. I need you nice and wet for me."

She played over Leah's clit and Leah felt it swell anew. Kayla moved between her legs and licked and sucked. Leah was teetering on the edge.

"Please," she said. "Please. Don't tease me."

She heard the buzzing then and felt the vibrator teasing her lower lips. She was teased only briefly before Kayla slid it inside her. In and out she moved it as Leah got closer and closer to the precipice. She needed more.

"Please."

Kayla placed the tip of the toy against her clit and Leah saw all the colors of the rainbows burst before her eyes as she came once, twice, and a third time.

Kayla untied her.

"Now, was that so bad?"

Leah just smiled at her.

"Now go for it. It's your turn. Do what you will."

Leah tied Kayla to the bed and walked around her, enjoying the view. She was all spread out and Leah drooled over the beauty between her legs. She climbed between them and licked her and sucked her juicy lips. She tasted so good that Leah could have stayed there all day, but she knew the rules. She picked up the vibrator that was lying by Kayla's hip. She turned it on. Curious, she ran the tip over Kayla's nipples.

"Oh, my God," Kayla said. "Oh yeah, that feels good."

Leah moved the toy and sucked Kayla's nipples. She tasted herself on them from the vibrator. She did taste good. Kayla was right. But that was beside the point. She needed to get Kayla off. She kissed down her belly and slipped the toy inside her. She moved it in and out while she sucked and licked her clit.

Kayla was moving all over, keeping up with Leah. Leah thrust harder and licked faster, and soon Kayla froze before relaxing on the bed.

"Damn, you're fun," Kayla said.

"So are you."

Leah untied Kayla and cuddled with her on the bed.

"You know I really enjoy you, Leah," Kayla said.

"Yeah?"

"But I'm not looking for a relationship. So I don't think you should message me again. I'd hate for you to get the wrong idea."

Leah felt deflated. She didn't want anything from Kayla but sex and she was embarrassed that Kayla thought otherwise.

"Oh, no worries," she said. "I know that. And I won't message you again. I just had a bad day and really needed someone to help me take my mind off it."

"And I'm glad I could help. But I mean it. No more, okay?"

"Okay."

Leah lay on the bed and watched Kayla get dressed. She wrapped a robe around her and walked Kayla to the door.

"Good luck in your search for experience," Kayla said.

"Thanks. And thanks for your help."

"My pleasure." She kissed Leah on the cheek and left.

Leah lay in bed basking in the afterglow of good sex. She could get used to this. Just before she fell asleep, her phone pinged. It was someone from Girl World asking her to meet up. Leah smiled as she drifted off.

CHAPTER TWELVE

Friday evening rolled around and Dillon was all set to meet yet another of Leah's dates. Her name was Cora, and Leah was all excited about getting back in the saddle again.

"I can't believe how many offers I've had since I updated my profile," she said. "I'm going to be busy for months to come. No pun intended."

Dillon forced a laugh. Leah was trying to be cute, but she knew she was nervous. She always was before a date. But that didn't mean Dillon had to laugh about Leah making women come. She hated the thought. One day she'd get the nerve to tell Leah that. She was sure. But for now, she kept her mouth shut.

Leah sat between her and Stephanie at the bar waiting for Cora to arrive.

"You don't have to wait," Leah said to Stephanie.

"Oh, I don't mind. I like to have a drink after work every so often."

"Okay, but don't feel obligated."

"I don't."

Dillon listened to the exchange and wondered what she heard in Leah's voice. Was it jealousy? Why on earth would she be jealous? She couldn't possibly know they'd slept together, and even if she did, what business was that of hers? Hell, she slept with someone new damned near every night.

"Let me see your phone again," Stephanie said.

Leah pulled up Cora's profile picture and showed it to them.

"I think she's here and headed your way," Stephanie said.

A tall woman with slicked back black hair approached the bar. She wore torn blue jeans and a leather jacket over a white T-shirt. Dillon fought the urge to stand taller than the woman and start a pissing contest. She didn't like this woman, who she knew both Stephanie and Leah would drool over.

"Hey there," the woman said. "I'm Cora."

"I'm Leah."

"Nice to meet you." She smiled, and her dark eyes glistened as her gaze roamed up and down Leah's body.

Dillon felt her skin crawl. She made a fist at her side. She really wanted to knock this Cora woman for a loop.

"Nice to meet you, too," Leah said. "And this is my best friend, Dillon, and one of our bartenders, Stephanie."

"Wow. I didn't know I was meeting the whole family."

"Just a couple of us." Dillon tried to hold her voice steady. She really didn't like Cora. But she didn't seem dangerous, so she couldn't really tell Leah not to go out with her.

"Well, you ready to get out of here?" Cora said. "I've got big plans for you tonight."

Dillon closed her eyes and tried to block out the conversation.

"Okay. I'll see you guys later," Leah said.

"See you," Stephanie said.

Dillon opened her eyes.

"Have fun." She made herself say.

When they were gone, Stephanie took the bar stool next to Dillon.

"Why do I get the feeling you don't like meeting Leah's dates?"

"What makes you say that?"

"Because you act like you hate it. And you're not your normal smooth self with them."

"They're not for me to impress. That's Leah's job. I just meet them to decide if they strike me as psycho killers. So far none of them have."

"But you don't like it."

"I don't know about meeting people on an app. It just seems kind of strange to me. That's all."

"Okay. If that's all it is. Because I worry about you."

"Me? I'm fine. But I am hungry. How about joining me for dinner?"

"Dinner?" Stephanie said. "Should I get my hopes up?"

"I would if I were you."

"So, where to for dinner?"

"Morgan's Steak House. I'm craving a thick steak and a baked potato."

"That sounds delicious. Shall I meet you there?"

"Sounds great. See you in a few."

Dillon was in a good mood when she pulled into the parking lot. Stephanie had beat her there, so with a spring in her step, Dillon walked inside to find her waiting with a buzzer in her hand.

"It's going to be fifteen minutes to a half hour. I put your name in. But I didn't know if you'd want to wait or not."

"Sure I do. Let's go to the bar."

The bar was crowded and Dillon left Stephanie at a table while she fought her way to the bar. She got a beer and a glass of wine and walked back to the table. There were two women talking to Stephanie. Dillon wondered who they were, but as she approached, she saw they were Sueann and Nadia.

"What's up, ladies?" Dillon asked as she handed Stephanie her wine.

"Nothing. We just saw Stephanie here and I recognized her from the bar so I thought we'd come over and say hi. What are you doing here? And where's Leah?"

"Leah is out on a date." Dillon watched Sueann closely, but saw no emotion at all pass over her face. "So Stephanie and I decided to spoil ourselves with some good food."

"That's great," Sueann said.

Just then, the buzzer in Stephanie's hand went off. Saved by the bell.

"If you'll excuse us," Dillon said. She guided Stephanie out of the bar and up to the hostess.

"I felt really bad," Stephanie said when they were seated. "But I don't remember either of those women from the bar."

"You wouldn't know one of them, but Sueann is Leah's ex."

"Oh no. Well, that explains why she asked where she is. Do you think telling her she's on a date made an impression?"

"No. Her expression didn't change. I don't think she cares. She's moved on."

"But then, so has Leah," Stephanie said.

"How do you figure?" Dillon forgot that Stephanie didn't know the whole story behind Leah's dates.

"Well, she goes on a lot of dates, so obviously she's over Sueann."

"Yeah. You're right."

Dillon searched for a way to change the subject. She didn't want to talk about Sueann or Leah and her dates. She wanted to focus on Stephanie and hopefully their night ahead.

"So, can I come over to your house after dinner?" she said.

Stephanie's whole face lit up.

"Are you serious?"

"I am. I mean, if it's okay."

"It's more than okay. I'd love it."

"I sure hope I don't piss you off and have you file sexual harassment against me or something."

"That's not going to happen. I want this as much as you do."

"Good. But maybe I should get it in writing, just in case."

The waitress came by then and Stephanie asked her for a pen after they'd ordered. She wrote on her cocktail napkin:

"I, Stephanie Wozniak, hereby swear never to file sexual harassment charges against Dillon Franklin."

She signed and dated it and handed it to Dillon.

"Put this in your pocket."

"I was just joking," Dillon said.

"I think we'll both feel better having it in writing, though."

"Okay."

They enjoyed their dinner together and kept the conversation light, mostly discussing different patrons at the bar. Finally, the check came and Dillon grabbed it.

"Hey, shouldn't this be Dutch?" Stephanie said.

"No. I've got this one."

"Can I leave the tip?"

"Nope."

Dillon was feeling her butch self and wanted to exert it. She was always butch, of that there was no doubt, but sometimes she felt it stronger than others. This was one of those times. And no way she was going to let Stephanie, her gorgeous date, pay for anything.

"Let's get out of here,"

Out in the parking lot, it took every ounce of self-control not to press Stephanie into her car door and kiss her. She looked wonderful that night, more beautiful than ever, and Dillon felt a need growing inside her that threatened to overtake reason. But she stood strong.

"So, I guess I'll follow you to your place?" she said.

"Sounds good. Go get in your truck. I'll be watching for you."

Dillon followed Stephanie to her house. Stephanie drove nice and slow, so there was no way Dillon could get lost. On one hand, she appreciated that, but on the other, she was in a hurry to get her home and undressed. Dillon had a surprise for her. She'd dressed appropriately for work that day, foreseeing the night ending like this.

Once inside the house, Stephanie got them each a drink and they sat next to each other on the couch. Dillon draped an arm over Stephanie's shoulders and held her somewhat close. They sipped their drinks and Stephanie snuggled closer.

"This is nice," she said.

"Later is going to be nicer."

Stephanie playfully slapped her chest.

"You're so bad."

"But you're so good. I can't wait to have some fun with you."

"Just to clarify, this is all still fun and games, right?"

"That's right. All fun and games. No commitment."

"Okay. Just checking."

"You sure you're okay with that?" Dillon said.

"Sure. You're so hot. I'd be a fool not to be."

"Okay. Just double-checking."

Dillon set her beer down and pulled Stephanie to her for a kiss. It was a long, luscious kiss that Dillon felt to her core. Her boxers were more than a little damp when the kiss ended.

"That's what I'm talkin' about," she said.

"Mm. Me, too."

They kissed again. And again. And finally, Dillon stood and offered her hand to Stephanie.

"Shall we take this to the bedroom?"

"We shall."

Once in her room, Stephanie started to unbutton Dillon's pants. Dillon gently took her wrists.

"Uh-uh," she said. "You first. I have a surprise for you."

Stephanie pulled her shirt over her head and unhooked her bra.

"Oh, yeah," Dillon said. "That's what I'm talkin' about."

She held one breast in her hands and bent to take the nipple in her mouth. She played her tongue over it before sucking it deep in her mouth.

"I can't stand much longer," Stephanie said. "I need to lie down."

"Take your slacks off."

Dillon watched appreciatively as Stephanie stepped out of her pants, then underwear. She was so gorgeous. Dillon planned to please her beyond words that night.

Stephanie climbed into bed and then turned her attention to Dillon.

"Your turn."

Dillon took off her shirt and undershirt. She watched Stephanie watching her. It was a turn-on, to be sure. She took off her jeans and slid her boxers down, revealing a strap-on she planned to use on Stephanie.

Stephanie's eyes went wide. She smiled broadly.

"Is that for me?"

"You know it."

"Come here." Stephanie turned the cock so it faced upward and gently tugged on it to bring Dillon onto the bed with her. "Get up here and let me at it."

"Easy there. All in due time."

"You look so hot with that thing on. I just want you to fuck my brains out with it."

"That's the plan."

Dillon lay on top of Stephanie and ground into her, pressing the tip of her dildo into Stephanie's clit. Stephanie moaned her appreciation. She wrapped her legs around Dillon and pulled her down into her.

Dillon kissed down Stephanie's body until she was between her legs. She licked her deep inside, reveling in her flavor.

"I feel your cock pressing against my leg," Stephanie said. "Please. I'm ready for it. Please use it on me."

Dillon carefully positioned herself above Stephanie and guided the dildo inside. She slid just the first inch inside then pulled out so only the tip was still in.

"Stop teasing me," Stephanie said. "Please."

Dillon lowered herself so the whole toy slipped inside Stephanie. Stephanie groaned as Dillon moved in and out of her. She thrust it deep, all the way to its base and Stephanie reached between them and rubbed her clit. In no time, Stephanie was crying out Dillon's name.

They lay together, joined by Dillon's cock, for several minutes. Eventually, Dillon withdrew and Stephanie smiled up at her.

"So, do you always wear that to work? Because now I'm going to look at you in a whole different light."

Dillon laughed.

"No. I had plans for tonight, so I wore it."

"Oh, you did, did you? And how come I didn't know about those plans in advance?"

"I thought I'd take a chance."

"I'm glad you did."

"Me, too."

Leah and Cora arrived home from dinner and Leah was incredibly turned on. Cora was different, but strong and sensual. Leah was sure she was in for a wonderful night. Even if she couldn't please her, she knew she'd have fun trying.

They skipped after-dinner drinks and Leah led Cora straight to her room.

"Just so you know," Cora said. "I'm much more into giving than I am receiving."

"But I need to learn how to give, too."

"I understand. But it might not be that easy because I'm not used to that."

"Are you stone?"

Cora laughed. It was a low rumble that Leah felt between her legs.

"Not exactly stone. Just that I'd rather give than receive. It's not that I don't enjoy receiving. It's just that I'm not used to it."

"Well, let's see what I can do," Leah said.

She took Cora's leather jacket off and set it on the chair. She took off her T-shirt and sports bra and ran her hands over her bare shoulders. Cora was sculpted so fine. She had an amazing body, and Leah couldn't wait to have her way with it. She didn't know what had come over her, though. She usually wanted to be taken first, but Cora had challenged her, so now she was going to do her best to get her off.

She slid her hands lower and played with Cora's small breasts. They were barely there, but they were perfect for Cora. She licked one nipple and then the other and smiled to herself as they responded.

Leah unbuttoned Cora's belt and undid the buttons on her jeans. She pulled them to the floor along with her boxers and held them while Cora stepped out of them. Her legs were long and muscular and Leah enjoyed kissing her way up the inside of one, stopping to nibble behind her knee.

"Sit on my bed, please," Leah said. "I'd like to taste you."

"I don't know…"

"Please. I need to try to make you feel good."

Cora sat on Leah's bed and Leah knelt between her legs. She buried her face in her pussy and licked her deep inside. She sucked as she licked and Cora gave a sharp intake of breath. Leah withdrew her tongue and replaced it with her fingers. This is what she had learned to do, so she thought she'd stick with it.

She lapped on Cora's clit and Cora grew tense. She knew she was close, so she sucked her clit and ran her tongue all over it. Cora's breathing was ragged, and Leah kept at her, thrusting her finger deeper and faster.

"Oh, God I'm close," Cora said. "So close."

Leah kept at it, determined to succeed.

"My asshole," Cora said.

"Hmm?"

"Fuck my asshole."

Leah stopped what she was doing and looked at Cora. Surely she had misheard.

"What did you say?"

"My ass," Cora said through gritted teeth. "That's all that will work."

Leah felt nauseous. She couldn't imagine doing that. It seemed too weird.

"I don't know."

"I'm not asking you to eat it. Just stick a finger in there. Come on. The mood is fading."

Leah stood.

"I'm sorry. I just can't."

"I brought gloves."

Gloves? Was she planning on doing that to Leah?

"I'm sorry, Cora."

Cora got off the bed and pulled her clothes on.

"You know, there are many ways to please a woman. Maybe you should learn all of them."

Leah heard the door slam. She locked it, feeling dirty, took a shower, and went to bed. She couldn't wait to call Dillon in the morning and tell her about this one.

CHAPTER THIRTEEN

Dillon woke up with Stephanie in her arms. She looked too good to pass up so Dillon skimmed her hand down Stephanie's body to where her legs met. She was still wet from the previous night's fun, and Dillon slid her fingers over her slick clit. Stephanie stirred, then woke up for real. She looked at Dillon.

"What do you think you're doing?"

"What does it feel like?"

"Didn't you get enough last night?"

"Never."

"Lucky for me you're insatiable," Stephanie said. She spread her legs wider.

Dillon slipped her fingers lower and massaged Stephanie's lips and opening. When she was sure she was wet enough, she slid them inside.

"God you feel good," Dillon said.

"So do you. Although, please be gentle. I'm a little sore from last night."

"Fair enough."

Dillon slowly moved her fingers in and out until Stephanie was moving around on the bed. Dillon swept her thumb over her clit, and Stephanie cried out and clamped hard around Dillon's fingers.

"Come up here," Stephanie said. "I want to have my way with you."

Dillon lay next to her, but then heard her phone ringing. She checked to see who was calling. Leah. Shit. She quickly got out of bed.

"Hey, kiddo."

"Hey. You up for breakfast? I can't wait to tell you about last night's adventures."

Dillon was overcome with guilt for being caught in bed with Stephanie. She tried to shake it off, but couldn't.

"Sure? Where and when?"

"I can pick you up in fifteen."

"No. I just got out of bed." It wasn't a lie. "Give me a half hour and you can pick me up."

"You just got out of bed? What's up with that?"

"I, um, I slept late. Look, just give me a half hour, okay?"

"Sure."

"So, I've got to go," Dillon said to Stephanie when she hung up the phone. She'd already begun dressing.

"Yeah, I got that. I guess I'll see you Monday?"

"You got it."

"And will you be wearing that cock again?"

"No." It came out harsher than she'd intended. "I mean, I don't know. We'll just have to wait and see."

"Fair enough." Stephanie gave her an odd look.

"What?" Dillon said.

"Nothing. You seem uptight."

"I'm not. I'm fine. Thanks for last night."

She kissed her on the cheek and let herself out. She cursed herself out as she drove home. How could she be so stupid? If she kept sleeping with Stephanie, eventually Leah would find out and then what would happen? Any chance she possibly had with her would be blown.

Dillon hurriedly showered and dressed and had just slipped her shoes on when Leah knocked on her door.

"Come in," Dillon called.

Leah walked in with a strange look on her face.

"What's up?"

"I don't know. Something seems off about your place."

"I don't know what," Dillon said. "I just took a shower, so maybe you're smelling that."

"No. I know what it is. You haven't made coffee."

Shit. Busted. She hadn't had time.

"I just figured I'd get some at the restaurant."

"Okay. If you say so."

"Now," Dillon said. "Where to?"

"Let's go to the Diner. I want grease."

"Okay. Let's go."

They arrived at the restaurant and placed their orders. Dillon was famished after twelve hours with Stephanie. She should have been walking on air after the awesome sex they'd had, but she felt horrible. She felt untrue to Leah. It was unreasonable, but it was how she felt and she couldn't help it.

"So," she said. She didn't want to have this conversation, but that's what Leah wanted so she might as well get it over with. "How was your date last night?"

"Oh, my God." Leah lowered her voice. "She wanted it in her butt."

Dillon almost spit out her coffee. She half wanted to laugh, but forced herself to remain serious. Sure, people did it like that. But Leah? There was no way.

"Wow," she said. "That must have been a shock."

"Yes, it was. And she wanted to do it to me, too."

"Wait a minute," Dillon said. "So you did it to her?"

"Of course not."

"Okay, so outside of that detail, how did it go?"

"Apparently, it's the only way she can come, so it wasn't a very successful night. And the ending left much to be desired. She yelled at me."

Dillon felt her muscles tighten. She wanted to find that Cora woman and punch her in the face.

"Why did she yell at you?"

"She said there are many ways to please a woman and I needed to be open to all of them. Or something like that."

Dillon sat back against the booth.

"Wow."

"Yeah. That's what I thought."

"I'm sorry, Leah."

"Thanks. I'm hoping she was an anomaly and I can get back on track."

"Maybe it's time for a break."

"No way. I want to be the best lover in town."

"Suit yourself."

"So tell me," Leah said. "Why did you sleep so late today? Were you at the bar late?"

"No. I just must have been tired."

"Okay. If you say so. But something about you seems off. I just can't put my finger on it."

"Don't waste your time. I'm fine."

Dillon spent the rest of the weekend working out and cleaning her house. Not that she expected company. She just liked a clean house. She thought about bringing Stephanie home to her house next time, but then chided herself that there would not be a next time. She couldn't do that again. No matter how much fun it had been.

Monday rolled around and she was at the bar first. Stephanie showed up shortly thereafter.

"Do you have a minute?" Stephanie said.

"Is this business related?"

"Yes."

"Then I have a minute. Come on in. Sit down."

"I was wondering if I could start coming in earlier. I mean, I know it means more pay, but I just don't see why you have to do so much of the setup when you have a perfectly capable employee."

"Let me talk with Leah. She's the money person. I'll let you know. But as long as you're here today, knock yourself out."

Stephanie smiled and Dillon felt her insides melt.

"Thanks."

She watched her walk out of the office and almost drooled at her body. Damn, she was fine. But Dillon couldn't touch that body again. No way, no how.

Leah came in just as Stephanie was leaving her office.

"What was she doing in the office?"

"She wanted to ask me a question."

"And what was that?"

"She wanted to know if she could come in every day a half hour earlier to open the bar so I don't have to do anything. I told her I'd have to ask you."

"Well, thank you for not just saying yes."

"Leah, I only hired her because we needed someone and you'd always liked her as a patron, so I figured you wouldn't mind if she could do the job. I really don't understand why you're so dead set against her."

"I'm not."

"Anyway," Dillon said. "I told her she could do it today, but we'd have to wait to hear from you. So think about it, huh?"

"I'll crunch the numbers."

"Are you in a foul mood today, or what?"

"I wasn't. Not until I came in here and found her in the office. I swear, sometimes I think there's something going on between you two."

"How do you figure?"

"I don't know. It's just a feeling."

"Well, lose it," Dillon said.

"I'm sorry. It's not like a romance thing. It's just like a conspiratorial vibe I get."

"We're not conspiring against you. Don't worry about it, okay?"

"Okay. On the upside, I have a date tonight."

"Oh really? Do tell." Dillon once again tried to muster up some happiness for Leah, but fell short. Oh well, Leah didn't know that and that was all that was important.

"Her name is Heather. She looks like a nice soft butch and she doesn't look like she has any weird kinks or fetishes or whatever." Dillon laughed. How could she tell? She looked at the picture and the profile and she seemed innocent enough.

"No. She looks normal enough." She handed the phone back to Leah.

"I think so. She'll be here at six. Is that okay?"

"Sure. I don't mind hanging around an extra hour."

"Thanks. You're the best, Dillon."

"No problem."

After helping with the lull before happy hour, Leah went home and showered and changed into a new dress she'd bought over the weekend. It was simple, yet brought out her eyes and hugged her figure. She knew she looked good and just hoped Heather thought so, too.

She came back to the bar a little before six to find Stephanie sitting with Dillon. Something about that angered her. Dillon was spending too much time with Stephanie. It wasn't right. Still, she had a date to focus on so she tried to remain upbeat.

"So you're both here to meet Heather, huh?" she said.

"I'm here to meet Heather. Stephanie is just here to keep me company."

"Isn't that nice of her?"

"I thought so."

Leah leaned on the bar between the two of them and ordered a dirty martini. She turned so her back was against the bar and surveyed the room.

"Have either of you seen Heather yet?"

"I have not," Dillon said.

"And I wouldn't know her if she walked in," Stephanie said.

"Oh, yeah." Leah showed her the picture on her phone.

"She's cute," Stephanie said.

"Hands off," Leah said.

"No worries there." She looked in the mirror. "I think she just arrived."

"Really?" Leah said and then spotted Heather approaching the other end of the bar. "That would be her all right. She's even cuter in person."

"As are you, I'm sure," Dillon said.

"You're biased. So what should I do? Should I wait until she sees me or go over to meet her?"

"I say you go say hi," Stephanie said.

"But then how would Dillon be able to vet her?"

"You can always bring her over here," Dillon said.

"Okay." Leah took a deep breath. "I'm going over."

She crossed over to the other end of the bar where Heather leaned against it drinking a beer.

"Heather?" Leah said.

She turned around. Leah was stunned by the depth of her brown eyes and the fullness of her lips.

"That's me. Leah?"

"Guilty as charged."

Heather's lips broke into a slow smile as she looked Leah up and down.

"So very nice to meet you."

"Likewise. Will you come with me? I have a friend I'd like you to meet."

"A friend? Like someone else who'll be with us tonight?"

"No. Nothing like that," Leah said. "Just a friend who wants to meet you."

"Oh. Like to make sure my intentions are pure. Well, they're not."

Leah laughed.

"And that's okay."

She took Heather's hand, strong and sure, and led her to where Dillon and Stephanie sat.

"Heather, I'd like you to meet my best friend, Dillon." She watched as they shook hands, each one sizing up the other. "And this is Stephanie."

Heather gave Stephanie the old once-over.

"You sure you don't want to join us tonight?" she said.

"No," Leah said emphatically. "It'll just be the two of us."

"Shame," Heather said.

Leah was not feeling good about the way the night might play out. She had had such high hopes, but they were falling fast.

"We should finish our drinks and head to the restaurant," Leah said.

"You got it." She downed her beer in one gulp. Leah took a few more sips of her drink and left the rest of it on the bar. She liked the feel of Heather's hand on her ass as they walked out into the night.

"So how does this work?" Heather said. "You ride with me? I ride with you?"

"I'll follow you to the restaurant and you follow me to my place."

"Sounds good. Though I wouldn't mind skipping the restaurant."

"You'll need fuel for the energy you're going to burn tonight."

"Ah yes. Good point."

Dinner was passed in pleasant conversation. Leah learned that Heather was an underwater filmmaker who was only in town for a few days on a break.

"Well, I'm glad you're in town now," Leah said. "How fortunate for me."

"For both of us, I hope."

After dinner, Heather followed Leah to her house. They went inside and Heather pulled Leah into her arms.

"You, my dear Leah, are a treasure. I'm so happy to have this night with you."

"I only hope I don't disappoint."

"You know, it's the journey that's the fun part. Not necessarily the end."

"But it's important to me that you finish."

"Well, let's make sure you finish first."

She kissed her then and Leah felt moisture pool between her legs. She kissed her back with all the pent up passion she was feeling. She pulled Heather close and pressed their chests together. Heather's breasts were so soft, and feeling them against hers left her dizzy with need.

"Let's take this to the bedroom," Heather said. "I've wanted you since the minute I saw you in the bar and I don't want to wait any longer to have you."

"That sounds fantastic to me. Come on."

She took Heather's hand and led her down the hall to the bedroom. Heather undressed Leah slowly, kissing every spot of skin as she laid it bare. Leah was on fire. She needed Heather desperately. When she was naked, she returned the favor, and soon they stood flesh against flesh. Leah thought she would implode from the heat.

"Take me," she said. "I need you now."

They fell onto the bed, limbs entwined and tongues dancing together. Leah's heart thudded. She couldn't remember the last time she'd been that turned on.

Heather slowly unwound her legs from Leah's and slipped her hand between hers. Leah moaned at the contact. She was more than ready for Heather. Heather stroked her gently at first, then more quickly as she pressed Leah's clit into her pubis. Leah closed her eyes and felt her world shatter. She slowly floated back to earth as she felt Heather's tongue on her again. She opened her eyes to see that Heather had positioned a knee on either side of her head. Her center hovered over her mouth.

Leah raised her head and sucked and licked everything she saw. Heather tasted amazing and she couldn't get enough of her. She gripped her hips while she licked around her opening before delving inside. She licked her way to her clit and tried to focus on pleasing her, but her attention was diverted as she approached her own orgasm. She kept licking and sucking Heather's clit, but not with the intensity she needed to. She closed her eyes as she felt her whole body tense. She was so close. Should she deny her own orgasm or give in? Then she had no choice. Heather hit just the right spot and Leah was catapulted into the atmosphere.

When she was able to focus again, she realized she hadn't finished her end of the deal so went back to playing with Heather's clit. Heather cried out and collapsed on top of her. She finally climbed off of her and came up to hold Leah.

"You knew what you were doing," she said.

"I've never done that before. It was hard to concentrate."

"I know. But it's fun, right?"

"Yeah it is. I may have to do that again."

"We can go right now if you want," Heather said.

"Okay."

"You on top this time."

Leah climbed on top of Heather and buried her face between her legs. She felt a little crude to have herself in Heather's face, but Heather tasted so good she soon forgot. Heather's tongue worked its magic in and on Leah, and soon she was calling her name, muffled by her pussy. She finished Heather off then and climbed off her.

They lay together for a while, then Heather finally spoke.

"Can I stay the night?"

"I don't think that would be a good idea."

"Why not? We could start tomorrow the way we finished tonight."

"Right. And you're on a break, so that would work for you. I, on the other hand, have to work tomorrow."

"Oh, that's too bad." She got up and dressed. "Well, if I'm ever in town again, can I ping you on Girl World?"

"Sure. I'd like that."

"Great. Take care, Leah."

"You, too, Heather."

She walked Heather to the door and let her out. She climbed back into bed and fell into a deep, satisfied slumber.

CHAPTER FOURTEEN

Friday morning, Dillon was at the bar first, as usual. She was playing on her computer when Stephanie showed up. "Have you heard from Leah if I can start coming in early?" "I haven't. And I haven't followed up with her. I'm sorry. I'll check today. For now, go ahead and make some coffee and start setting up."

Soon Dillon smelled the fresh coffee and went out to get a cup. She sat at the bar and watched Stephanie getting things ready. She felt her whole body respond to her. She knew she couldn't have her again. Or rather, she shouldn't, but she didn't know if she was strong enough.

Maybe after work, she'd take Leah out to dinner. That would be better than sleeping with Stephanie again. And maybe, just maybe, she'd ask Leah to go out again. For more than dinner. A real date, maybe. But she knew she wouldn't. It was all a fantasy. Except dinner. She made up her mind to ask her to dinner before she did anything stupid and asked Stephanie out.

She went back into the office so she would quit drooling over Stephanie, and Leah finally came in.

"How's it goin' today?" Dillon said.

"Why is Stephanie here?"

"She came by to see if you'd crunched the numbers yet on her coming in early. I told her I'd talk to you and then told her to go ahead and get things set up."

"Okay. Is that coffee fresh?"

"Very."

Leah left to get a cup of coffee and Dillon watched her leave the room. Regardless of what she felt for Stephanie, it couldn't compare to what she felt for Leah. Stephanie was sex. That was it. Leah was so much deeper.

Dillon looked up when the office door opened to see Leah walking in with a cup of coffee.

"This is really good," she said.

"Stephanie made it. I think she brings her own from home."

"She can't do that. We pay for coffee."

"Maybe we should switch brands. I'll look into costs and get back to you."

"Sounds good."

"So how are you today?" Dillon asked again.

"I'm great. I have another date tonight."

"Wow. You're just getting them left and right. I thought they would slow down eventually." Or hopefully, which she did not add.

"Tonight I have a date with Christa. She looks kind of rough, but I think I've had a taste of everything at this point, so I think I can handle her."

"I hope so. Let me see her pic."

Leah handed her phone over and Dillon stared at the woman in the photo. She didn't look that rough. She seemed a little older, but that was all she noticed. She had a lot of gray in her otherwise brown hair, which she wore cropped short.

"She looks nice enough to me," Dillon said.

"Yeah. She's attractive enough. Something about her just screams rough around the edges to me."

"I don't see it. I'm sure you'll have fun. What time will she be here?"

"Six. Sorry."

"It's Friday night. I don't mind hanging out an hour later. It'll be nice to have a few beers after work."

"Will Stephanie be joining you?"

Oh, crap. She seriously seemed to be onto them.

"Probably," Dillon said nonchalantly.

"Okay. You two sure seem to get along."

"She's a nice person. You should get that chip off your shoulder and take a chance getting to know her."

"I work with her every afternoon," Leah said. "I know she's nice enough."

"Good."

Dillon heard the bell ring announcing the arrival of a customer. She knew Stephanie could handle it, but she went behind the bar, just in case. She and Stephanie chatted with the regulars and soon it was lunchtime. The rush was heavier than usual, and many people stayed after lunch to drink their Friday afternoon away.

Leah came out to relieve Dillon at two, but Dillon shooed her away. She was having fun and knew Leah had to get ready for her date.

"My date's not for another four hours," Leah said.

"Still. Go on. Seriously. We've got this."

"Okay. If you insist. Maybe I'll go buy a new dress."

"There you go," Dillon said.

"So I'll see you at six?"

"I'll be here."

She watched Leah walk out and fought the nausea in her stomach. She worried for her. She hated what she was doing, but she worried every single time that the person she was meeting might be some kind of axe murderer. Maybe she was overreacting, but she couldn't help it.

She felt Stephanie's warm breath in her ear.

"So Leah has another date tonight, huh?"

Dillon waited until her body relaxed again before she tried to speak.

"Yep. She'll be here at six."

"Do you want me to hang with you after work?"

"I'd like that. And then maybe we can get some dinner after?"

The words were out before she could stop them. Damn her hormones.

"And after?"

Dillon couldn't help it. She smiled a smile that she was sure left no doubt in Stephanie's mind about what she wanted to do after. The afternoon passed quickly with the patrons in a wonderful mood. Dillon had fun with all of them and worked her butt off until the evening crew arrived at five. Once they had balanced their till, she put the money in the safe in the office and sat at the bar with a beer.

Stephanie sat next to her sipping her wine.

"I'm looking forward to dinner," she said. "I'm starving."

"We worked hard this afternoon. You should be hungry."

"I'm looking forward to dessert, too."

"Me, too."

Dillon was on her third beer and Stephanie her second glass of wine when Leah came in looking stunning in a new green dress. It took a moment for Dillon to find her words.

"You look amazing," she said. "Simply amazing."

"Why, thank you. I'm glad you like it."

She turned around to show off the low-cut back of the dress. Dillon could barely breathe. She wanted to be the one to unzip the dress, to feel the soft skin on her back. She shook herself out of it.

"Very nice."

"Thanks. Is Christa here?"

"Not yet."

Dillon noticed that Leah hadn't said a word to Stephanie.

"You want to show Stephanie her picture so we can all keep an eye out for her?"

Leah passed her phone over to Stephanie.

"She's cute," Stephanie said.

"Yep. I'm looking forward to tonight."

"I think she's here," Dillon said. "She's sitting at a table in the corner. I didn't see her come in."

Leah turned and surveyed the bar.

"Are you sure that's her?"

"Pretty sure," Dillon said.

Dillon watched the woman in the mirror as she approached.

"Oh, shit. Here she comes," Leah said. "Are you sure I look okay?"

"You look great," Stephanie said. "Just relax."

Christa walked up and stood in front of Leah.

"Leah, I presume?"

"That's me. Christa?"

"Yep. Wow, you look much better in person than you do in your profile."

"Thanks? I think?"

Christa laughed.

"Oh, no worries," she said. "Your profile pic is great, but you're even more beautiful in person."

Dillon watched Leah blush. She turned away from them. Until she felt Leah's soft, warm hand on her arm. She turned back.

"Christa, this is my best friend, Dillon."

Christa extended her hand and Dillon ruefully shook it.

"Nice to meet you Dillon. Glad someone is watching over Leah making sure no weirdo is taking her home."

"That's my job indeed."

"Well, do I pass muster?"

"Yep. But if you hurt her, know it's me you'll be dealing with."

"That's the glory of these one-shot deals isn't it?" Christa said. "No way to get hurt."

"I think you know what I mean."

"I do. I'll take good care of her." She turned to Leah. "Shall we?"

They left the bar and Dillon turned to Stephanie.

"You about ready to get out of here?"

"I thought you'd never ask."

Dillon drove to her favorite steak house with Stephanie close behind. Her thoughts were on what would happen after dinner; how she would enjoy Stephanie's body and all it had to offer.

When Stephanie parked next to her, Dillon got out of her car and pressed Stephanie into her car door.

"I can't wait until after dinner. I need a taste now," she said. She kissed Stephanie hard and deep and felt Stephanie's kiss in return.

"Dillon!" She heard Leah's voice. "Dillon Franklin! What the hell do you think you're doing?"

Shit! Shit, shit, shit. This wasn't good. It wasn't good at all. "Leah?"

"Yes, Leah. What the hell do you think you're doing making out with an employee?"

"It's not like it looks."

"Oh no? Then what is it?"

Leah was livid. She'd suspected they were close, but hadn't let her brain go to how close they really were. She was so upset, she didn't even know if she could go through with her date with Christa.

"Look," Dillon said. "I'm sorry. We'll go somewhere else."

"That doesn't change the fact that you're sleeping together."

"It was just a kiss, Leah."

"It was more than just a kiss and you know it. How could I have been so blind? I knew there was something between you two. I just wouldn't let myself believe it. There were those lingering glances and always hanging at the bar after your shift."

"We hung at the bar after our shifts per your request."

"Don't try to be indignant. You've been caught red-handed."

"Okay. Look, I'm sorry. We'll go our separate ways now and let you have your evening."

"I don't know if I even want to have my evening now. I think you two spoiled it for me."

"Are you serious?" Christa said. "Because I know the perfect thing to get your mind off this."

"Well, I've certainly lost my appetite," Leah said.

"We're leaving," Dillon said, and Leah watched them get into their separate vehicles and drive off. Would they meet up somewhere else? Probably. The thought made her ill.

"So, can I ask you a question?" Christa said.

"What's that?"

"Why are you so upset? Are you into Dillon or something?"

"God no. She's my best friend. But she shouldn't be sleeping with the staff."

"Still. I think you overreacted."

Leah thought about it. Had she overreacted? No. She'd never been comfortable with Stephanie, and now that she knew they were an item, she liked her even less. How dare Dillon?

"Are you sure you don't want dinner?"

"I don't know. I don't know if I'm going to be very good company tonight," Leah said.

"Well, let's at least have drinks. If we get along, we can always reschedule tonight."

"That sounds fair."

They walked into the restaurant and cut through the crowd to the bar. Leah chose a seat while Christa bought them drinks. When she handed Leah's to her, she took a drink.

"Wow! That's strong."

"I ordered you a double. I thought you might need it."

"So you're going to get me drunk and take advantage of me?"

"No," Christa said. "I just thought you might need it. Honest."

"I'm sorry for the scene I made."

"I'm not sure I understand, but you're forgiven."

"Dillon and I own The Kitty. Stephanie is an employee. Do you know what kind of trouble Dillon was setting us up for?"

"Looked to me like she was just having a bit of fun. Stephanie didn't seem to mind it at all."

"Still. She could cause problems if she wanted to. Dillon obviously wasn't thinking."

They finished their drinks and Christa ordered them two more.

"This one isn't a double. I promise," she said.

Leah took a sip. Much better.

"So are you starting to relax?" Christa said.

"A little. But I'm sorry. I don't think I can go home with you tonight. I'm still too upset."

"Bummer for me. Maybe some other time?"

"Sure. Definitely."

"Is your appetite back? We don't need to eat steak and lobster, but maybe some appetizers to soak up the drinks?"

"Sure." Leah didn't want to come off as a complete bitch, but she really just wanted to go home and be alone. Still, appetizers couldn't hurt.

They ordered some apps and ate them at their table in the bar area. When they were gone, Leah stood.

"I really am sorry, Christa. I like you a lot. But the mood was spoiled for me."

"And that's okay. But do me a favor, okay? You need to examine your feelings for Dillon. I think there's more there than you let yourself believe."

"I appreciate that, but I know how I feel. She's just a friend. A good friend, but a friend nonetheless. I have no romantic feelings for her."

They said good night and Leah drove home alone. She was grateful for the quiet of her house. The noisy bar and conversations with Christa hadn't let her truly process what she'd seen. And Dillon hadn't tried to deny that they were sleeping together. Sure, she'd said it was just a kiss, but no one kisses like that unless they expect more to come.

Leah ran a bath and slid into it. She hoped it would relieve some of the tension that filled her body. She lay back and closed her eyes and breathed deep of the lavender scented bath oil. She willed herself to calm down, but the pictures of Dillon and Stephanie kept flowing through her brain. She finally drained the water, took a shower, and went to bed. But sleep escaped her.

Monday morning, she texted Dillon to let her know she wouldn't be in to work. Let her think she'd had such a good weekend with Christa that she couldn't make it. And she texted her because she was still too upset to talk to her.

Dillon texted right back.

Are you ok?

I'm fine. Just taking a day off. You two should be fine without me.

Leah, please.

Leave me alone. I'm taking a day off and I'm through talking to you.

She tossed her phone on the other side of the bed. Ugh. Now she had a whole day to think about what she'd seen. As if the weekend hadn't been long enough. At least she didn't have to be there with them. Fucking lovebirds. How many times had they slept together? Did they have feelings for each other? She had so many questions and no answers. And no way to get answers. Unless she confronted Dillon point-blank. Was she bold enough to do that?

She spent the day cleaning her house and was just getting in the shower when she heard her phone ring. She looked at it. Dillon. Did she dare answer it?

"Hello?" She said.

"Leah. Look. I'm, um, I'm sorry about Friday."

"Sorry you got caught, you mean?"

"Sorry about my lapse in judgment. I was wondering if maybe you and I could go to dinner tonight to kind of clear the air. That is unless you've got a date or something."

"I don't have a date. Pick me up in fifteen. But, Dillon?"

"Yeah?"

"Don't expect me to be happy to see you."

CHAPTER FIFTEEN

Dillon had a beer at the bar. Stephanie joined her with a glass of wine. It had been a long day at the bar, with Dillon feeling awkward around Stephanie. Stephanie had texted her later Friday night and asked her to come over, but Dillon had declined. It wasn't fair for Stephanie to be put in the middle and Dillon knew that, but that's where she'd ended up and Dillon wasn't sure how to apologize without letting her feelings for Leah show.

"So what are you doing tonight?" Stephanie said.

"I'm taking Leah to dinner."

"Are you serious? After the way she freaked out on us? And then didn't show up to work today? You're still taking her to dinner?"

"I just think we need to clear the air."

"And I think you're being too nice."

"Stephanie, please."

"Please what?"

"You don't understand."

"Then educate me. What don't I understand?"

How to proceed? To explain to her that she was in love with Leah and couldn't stand to have her mad at her?

"We just need to get along if we're going to run this business together, so we need to talk sometime. Obviously, I had to make the first move. She wasn't going to."

"And I think she should have made the first move. She's the one that freaked out. And what's with all her dates anyway? That Christa woman said they were a one-time thing. Is Leah really just sleeping around? You know what I think? I think Leah has feelings for you and just won't admit it."

"That's enough, Stephanie." Dillon fought hard to control her temper. Leah didn't have feelings for her. That was the whole problem.

"Suit yourself. Maybe you're the one with feelings for her. Have you ever thought about that?"

"I'm serious, Stephanie. This subject is closed."

"I think I hit a nerve." She stood, finished the last drop of wine, and left the bar.

Dillon checked the clock. She only had five minutes to get to Leah's. She downed her beer and drove off. She sat in her truck in front of Leah's house for just a moment to gather herself before she got out and walked to the door. She had Leah's spare key in her pocket, just in case she didn't answer the door.

But Leah answered, looking stunning in faded jeans and a worn T-shirt.

"Let's go," she said.

"Aren't you even going to invite me in?"

"No. I'd feel like my house was unclean with you in it. And I just scrubbed it today. So, no. I'm not inviting you in. I'm letting you buy me dinner, though I'm not sure why."

They drove in silence to Leah's favorite Mexican food restaurant. They were greeted by name and shown to their usual table. Dillon ordered them each a margarita, took a deep breath, and began.

"Look, Leah. I think we need to clear the air. We need to talk about what happened. And we need to be able to move on."

"Move on? You've been fucking Stephanie and you want me to just move on?"

"To be honest, I don't know where this anger is coming from. Yes, she's an employee. But I had her sign that there would be no repercussions."

"Are you serious?"

"Yes."

"So, what? She was just an easy lay?" She sounded incredulous.

"Who are you to talk about that? What the hell have you been doing for the past couple of months?"

"That's different."

"How? Please, I'd like to know how."

"Mine was for a reason," Leah said.

"And mine wasn't? For God's sake, do you think I'm supposed to live a celibate lifestyle? I'm human, too, you know."

"You've never complained about it before."

"How long do you think it had been since I'd had sex?"

She sat back in her booth while the waitress dropped off their drinks.

"How am I supposed to know?"

"I bet you do know," Dillon said. "I bet you know exactly when. We used to be tight. We used to do things together. We used to know everything each other was doing."

"You're the one who changed that. I've been honest about my meetings with women from Girl World. You're the one fucking Stephanie in secret."

"No. You've been too consumed with sleeping with every woman around to pay any attention to me or what I've been doing. You're the one who's changed, and I don't think I like it."

"Maybe dinner wasn't a good idea." Leah reached for her purse.

"No, Leah. Please stay. Please?"

Leah looked at her for a long minute.

"Fine. But can we stop fighting?"

"Sure."

"And will you stop sleeping with Stephanie?"

"Will you stop meeting women on Girl World?"

"What's that got to do with it?" Leah said.

"It's no fair for you to get sex once or twice a week and me to never get it. I don't think that's right."

"But does it have to be Stephanie?"

"I don't want to sleep around, Leah. That's not my thing. Stephanie is available for fun and games. There's no strings attached. No emotions involved. It's just someone to be with. I can't believe you would deny me that."

Leah was silent for a long while. She sipped her margarita. Dillon sat on pins and needles waiting for an answer.

"I guess what you say makes sense," Leah said at last. "But I'm not happy about it."

"Okay. Now what about you and app dating?"

"Oh, that's not going to stop."

"Okay. So we're each allowed to find satisfaction where we can. We can talk about it with each other, though. I'm glad I don't have to sneak around with Stephanie anymore."

"So, how often do you sleep with her?"

"Less than once a week. Really. Just once in a while. It's not a regular thing."

"That would make me feel better. But I don't know if I believe you."

"It's true. We're not like an item or anything. It's a once in a while kind of thing."

Dinner was served then and they both ate.

"That was good," Leah said. "I have to be honest, I didn't think I'd be able to eat when you asked me to dinner."

"Well, I'm glad you're feeling better."

"Can I ask for a favor?"

Dillon was hesitant.

"What's that?"

"Don't make me feel like a third wheel at work. I'd really hate that."

"Kiddo, we're not an item. I mean that. You shouldn't feel uncomfortable."

"But I will. I know that."

"Then that's on you," Dillon said. "We're just going to act like two people doing our jobs. You should be fine."

"Okay. And you'll be happy to know I crunched the numbers and she can come in a half hour early every day."

"She'll be happy to know that. It doesn't matter to me. Except it means less work for me, which is always good."

"I can't believe I'm saying it's okay for you to keep seeing her."

"You don't have to. All you have to do is quit that app dating and I'll quit sleeping with Stephanie. It's hard to hear about all your adventures, you know? It makes me want to give it a try again. I just happened to try with Stephanie and I'm sorry that upset you."

Dillon saw tears well up in Leah's eyes.

"I thought you understood how important my app dating is for me."

"I do. I really do. But it made me realize I hadn't had sex in a very long time and I started wanting it. That's all."

"Okay. I guess I get it."

"Good. Now, you want to go back to my place for a nightcap?"

"No. I think I've had enough. Why don't you drop me off at my place?"

When they were in front of Leah's house, Dillon reached out and put her hand on Leah's arm.

"So, will we see you at work tomorrow?"

"Yes. I'll be there."

"Excellent. See you then."

She drove off feeling somewhat better. At least they'd talked. She just wished, as always, that she could tell Leah how she felt about her. But she knew she'd freak out again and there was the bar to consider. Would Leah still want to co-own the bar with her if she knew she was in love with her? She doubted it. So, in that sense, nothing was resolved, but at least Leah was okay with her sleeping with Stephanie. If only Stephanie would go for it again. Dillon pulled into her driveway thinking how messed up her life really was.

❖

Leah stripped out of her clothes and threw them in the washer. They smelled like Mexican food. She walked down the hall and sank into a nice warm bath. Her mind was jumbled. She couldn't believe she'd said it was okay for Dillon to continue to sleep with Stephanie. But then, what right did she really have to say no? They were both adults. Consenting adults, even.

And why was Dillon so dead set against her app dating? She'd been against it from the beginning, but she seemed almost angry about it now. What was that about?

Her bath grew tepid, and she showered and climbed into bed. It was early, but she was exhausted. And in the morning she had to face the happy couple at the bar.

Morning came too early. She had had strange dreams all night about Dillon and her. They'd become an item. They were very bizarre, yet almost realistic. She was aroused to the point of pain. She was throbbing and needed relief. She closed her eyes and slid her hand between her legs. She was surprised at how wet she was. She teased her opening, then slid her fingers inside. She slipped them over her swollen clit and finally cried out as she came once and then again. And the whole time she'd thought of Dillon. What was up with that?

She showered and dressed, then headed to work. She arrived before Dillon or Stephanie, as was her hope. She put on a pot of coffee and settled into her chair in the office to start work on the day's accounting. She was concentrating hard when the office door opened and she looked up to see Dillon standing there.

"Good morning," Leah said.

"Is it? I mean, we're really good?"

Leah thought of her dreams the night before and felt a blush creep over her face.

"Yep. We're great."

"Most excellent. I brought doughnuts. As kind of a peace offering," Dillon said.

"Yum. I haven't eaten yet this morning. Doughnuts sound amazing."

Dillon set the box on her desk and opened it.

"You first," she said.

Leah chose the apple fritter, which was her all-time favorite.

"Oh, my God," she said between mouthfuls. "You're the best, Dillon."

"Thanks."

There was a knock on the door and Stephanie poked her head in.

Leah felt the anger rise inside her. She fought to tamp it down and remain cool. They all had to work together. Unless she chose to fire Stephanie, which was tempting, but it wouldn't be fair to Dillon.

"We have doughnuts for breakfast," Leah said as pleasantly as she could. "Help yourself."

"Thanks, but I'm not hungry right now. Maybe later?"

"Sure. Oh, and I don't know if Dillon told you or not, but I crunched the numbers and you're welcome to come in a half hour early every day if you want."

"I'd like that very much. Thank you."

"Good. So go ahead and get started," Leah said.

"Right. I'm on it."

She left the office and Leah looked over to see Dillon watching her.

"What?" she said.

"That took a lot of effort. Being nice to her, I mean. Is it always going to be that hard for you?"

"Give me time, Dillon. I'm trying."

"Okay."

They sat there working when Leah's phone pinged. She looked at it to see a message from Christa.

"You want to try again tonight?"

"Who's that?" Dillon said.

"It's Christa. She wants to get together again tonight."

"Are you going to do it?"

"I think so. She kind of got the short end of the stick that night."

"Yeah. I suppose so. She really didn't need to see our blowup." Leah typed back to her.

"Sure. Meet me at the bar at six?"

"I'll be there."

"So what's the plan?" Dillon said.

"We're meeting here at six. You don't have to wait around if you don't want to."

"Okay. I probably won't."

Leah finished her accounting and set off to run her daily errands for the bar. She got back and sat in the office until it was her turn to work with Stephanie behind the bar. It wasn't going to be easy, but she had to do it. She took a deep breath to steel herself, then stepped out of the office.

"I'm going to have lunch." Dillon went into the kitchen to make herself a burger. Leah wondered once again how she could eat all she did and still keep her body. She was tall and lean without an ounce of fat on her. Leah thought again of her dreams of the previous night. She shook her head. She didn't need to think about them at work.

The afternoon was slow, and Leah was anxious to get out of there to get ready to meet Christa.

"I think I've got a handle on this if you would rather do office work," Stephanie said.

"No. I'm here to help. Just in case."

"Okay."

She watched Stephanie flirt with all the customers that came in, and she suddenly understood Dillon's attraction to her. She was nice looking, not Leah's type, but for a butch like Dillon, she'd be a prime catch. And she was fun and flirtatious. No wonder Dillon fell prey to her charms.

When her shift ended, Leah went home and got ready for her date. She was back at the bar at five forty-five, and there were very few people there. She sat at the bar and nursed her dirty martini until Christa got there.

"You ready to try again?" she heard Christa before she saw her.

"I am."

"Good. At least this time, we won't have any surprises, will we?"

"Nope."

They set off to the restaurant where they chatted easily. Leah really liked Christa.

"I'm really sorry about our last date," she said.

"It's forgotten."

"Good."

They arrived at Leah's house, and she took Christa's hand and led her down the hall to her bedroom. She didn't want to wait a moment more to have her and be had by her.

Christa proved to be a skilled lover, using her fingers and tongue to take Leah over the edge time and time again. And then it was Leah's turn. She propped herself up on her elbow and gazed longingly at Christa's body.

"I love your body," she said.

"It's here for you to love. Don't stare too long, dear. I'm ready for you."

Leah had an idea. Even though Christa had just finished with her, she still wanted more. She knew she was being greedy, but she couldn't help it. She slipped her fingers inside Christa as deep as she could. She withdrew them then thrust them in again. Christa arched up, meeting each one. Leah moved them to her clit and rubbed it until Christa cried out.

Then she positioned herself so her pussy was just over Christa's face and she buried her own face between Christa's legs. She felt Christa's tongue on her, and she fought to maintain her focus on Christa. It wasn't easy, but she fought not to come until she'd gotten Christa off. It was a losing battle, though. She came hard just before Christa did as well.

They lay together after and Leah almost fell asleep. "I guess I should get going now, huh?" Christa said.

"Yeah. Probably."

"You know, you're a lot of fun. No one should tell you you don't know how to please a woman. You were awesome."

"Thanks. I needed to hear that."

CHAPTER SIXTEEN

Dillon was sitting at home watching television thinking about Leah off with Christa. She felt alone and didn't like it. She used to be fine spending time by herself, but at the moment, she wanted company. She called Stephanie.

"Hello?"

"Hey, Stephanie."

"Dillon? What's up?"

"Look, I never apologized for the way things went down Friday night."

"You were right the other night. It was none of my business. Obviously, there's something between the two of you and it's got nothing to do with me. Except I happened to be sleeping with you."

"Okay. Well, anyway. I was wondering if I could come over."

"What? Now?"

"Yeah. Would that be okay?"

There was a long pause. Dillon thought Stephanie may have hung up.

"Are you there?"

"Yeah, I'm here. You know I'd love to have you come over, but I don't want to complicate things with you and Leah."

Dillon laughed. As if they could be more complicated.

"You won't. I promise."

"Okay. Come on over."

Dillon drove over and knocked on the door. Stephanie opened the door in a short satin kimono. Her mouth went dry. Stephanie was stunning. And clearly ready for her.

"Did you bring any special treat with you?" Stephanie said.

"Not this time."

"Bummer. Come on in."

Dillon walked in and ran her hand down Stephanie's arm. Her robe was so silky soft, but Dillon couldn't wait to get her out of it.

"You want a beer?" Stephanie said.

"Sure." She didn't really. She wanted to skip to the good stuff, but she figured she'd play it somewhat cool.

Stephanie left the room to get them drinks. Her robe barely covered her ass and Dillon clenched her fist in an effort to calm her desire. Stephanie was back with a beer for her and a glass of wine for herself. She sat next to Dillon, tucking her feet up underneath her on the couch. Dillon tried not to stare between her legs, where she knew she could just barely see her pussy.

She took a long drink from her beer to quench her still dry mouth. It helped a little.

"So, what have you been doing this evening?" Stephanie said.

"Watching TV. What about you?"

"I was taking a bath when you called."

"Ah. That explains the outfit."

"I wanted to look nice for you."

"Well, you certainly do," Dillon said. "And I appreciate it."

"You're welcome."

She snuggled up against Dillon, who wrapped her arm around her shoulders. She kissed the top of Stephanie's head.

"You're so beautiful," she said.

"I'm glad you think so. I happen to think you're pretty handsome."

"That's a good thing."

She leaned in and brushed her lips over Stephanie's.

"That was nice," Stephanie said.

"Yeah it was. I like kissing you."

"You're the best kisser."

"I think you're pretty good at it yourself," Dillon said.

She took another long pull off her beer. She was burning up inside, and even the cold beer could do nothing to assuage it. She rested her hand on Stephanie's exposed thigh. She couldn't wait to run her hand up her smooth skin to find her wet center. Patience. All in good time.

"I think having a drink was a bad idea," Stephanie said.

"Why's that?"

"Because I'd rather have you in my room already."

"We'll get there. You know we will."

She took another gulp. She still had half a beer left, and Stephanie had barely touched her wine.

"You'd better start on that wine, though. Or we won't make it."

"I don't think I'm thirsty. At least not for wine. Put your beer down. Come on. I need you now."

Dillon walked with her to her room, and they stood together next to the bed. Dillon slid the shoulder of Stephanie's robe down and kissed and nibbled her bare skin. She tasted clean and fresh, of vanilla and almonds. She nuzzled her neck behind her ear and kissed back to her shoulder.

"You're making me crazy," Stephanie said.

"What do you think you're doing to me in this robe?"

She slid her other shoulder down and repeated her actions on the other side. When she couldn't stand it any longer, she untied the belt and let the robe fall to the ground. Stephanie stood there looking stunning wearing only what nature gave her. She was beautiful.

"My God. I can't get over how hot you are."

"I think you're overdressed," Stephanie said. She unbuckled Dillon's belt and unbuttoned her jeans. She slid them and her boxers down her legs. Dillon stepped out of them and Stephanie stayed on the ground, resting her cheek on Dillon's inner thigh. She knelt higher and ran her tongue over Dillon.

"Whoa, babe. Ladies first."

"But you're so delicious. I couldn't resist just a taste."

"Okay, but now get up on that bed. I'm going to have you every which way I can."

She quickly stripped out of her shirt and undershirt and joined Stephanie. She lay on top of her and kissed her hard and deep. Stephanie wrapped her legs around her. Dillon could feel the heat rising from her. She was dizzy with need. She rolled off her and slid her hand down to where her legs met. She was hot and tight, and Dillon easily slipped her fingers inside.

"More, baby. I need more," Stephanie said.

Dillon slipped another finger and knew Stephanie wouldn't be able to take any more. She had her filled with three fingers, more than she'd ever used on her, and fucked her nice and slowly while she twisted her hand as she moved it in and out.

"Oh dear God," Stephanie said. "Oh, my God, you feel good."

Dillon lowered her mouth and sucked Stephanie's pert nipple while she continued to please her. Stephanie grabbed her wrist to hold her in place as she rode the orgasms that washed over her.

And then it was Dillon's turn. She was so wet and ready, she was sure she would come at Stephanie's first touch. She gritted her teeth when she felt Stephanie slide over her swollen clit and delve inside her. She bucked off the bed, meeting every thrust. Stephanie knew how to please her. She was touching all her special spots inside. And then she was rubbing her clit. Slowly at first, just enough to drive Dillon wild. Then, she rubbed faster and Dillon felt her energy coalesce inside her center. She closed her eyes and let out a low, guttural moan as the energy burst forth, spreading white heat throughout her body.

She held Stephanie until she heard Stephanie's breathing slow into a steady rhythm. Shit. She couldn't sleep there. She needed to get going. She tried to ease her arm out from under her.

"Mm," Stephanie said.

"Hey, Stephanie? I need to get going."

"Hmm?" She opened her eyes. "I'm sorry. I didn't mean to fall asleep."

"It's okay. But I do have to go. I'll see you in the morning."

❖

Dillon woke in the morning smiling. Her body was relaxed and she could feel everywhere Stephanie had touched the night before. She stretched, got out of bed, and turned her coffee on. She took a nice, hot shower, then dressed for the day. She had some coffee then left for the bar, bracing herself for news of how Leah's date had gone. She really hoped she didn't have to hear details. Leah could just tell her if it went well or not and she'd be happy.

She got there first and unlocked the delivery door in the back and let herself in. She turned on the coffee and went to the office. She was checking on her order of T-shirts for the softball team when she heard a knock on the door.

"Come in," she said.

Stephanie walked in.

"What's up?" Dillon said.

"I just wanted to thank you for last night. I had a really good time."

"Me, too. We'll have to do it again. Soon."

"That sounds good to me."

Leah let herself in the front door of the bar. The bells jingled as she entered. She walked back to the office to find Dillon talking to Stephanie.

"Am I interrupting?" she said.

"Nope. I was just saying good morning," Stephanie said. "I'm off to work now."

She left the office. Leah stood with her arms crossed glaring at Dillon.

"What?" Dillon said.

"What did I ask?"

"Huh? What do you mean?"

"I asked that I not be made to feel like a third wheel in my own bar."

"You shouldn't feel like a third wheel. Or if you do, you're bringing it on yourself. She just said good morning and let me know she was here."

"If you're so innocent, why are you so defensive?"

"I'm not going to have this discussion. It's over. She came in to say good morning and that was all. If you're going to get all paranoid every time we talk, well, you just need to get over it is all."

Leah sat in her chair but kept her gaze on Dillon.

"Are you sure?" she said.

"I'm sure."

"Okay." Leah relaxed. "Do you want to hear about my date last night?"

"Sure. How'd it go with Christa?"

"It went amazingly well. I'm really getting the hang of this. And I'm able to mix things up now and still get women off. I've come so far, Dillon."

"That's great. When's your next date?"

"I don't have one planned yet. No one has contacted me. Hopefully soon though. I've found it's a lot of fun to please a woman."

"I'd have to agree."

"Don't remind me," Leah said.

Dillon just looked at her.

It was time for Dillon to go out to work behind the bar, and Leah was way behind on her morning duties. She finished entering numbers in their accounting program then took off to run her errands. She came back just before the lunch rush started and saw Dillon and Stephanie talking easily behind the bar. She quelled the fit of jealousy she felt rising within her. She had no reason to be upset.

She suddenly had an idea. She waited until after the lunch rush and broached the subject to Dillon and Stephanie.

"Look, I feel like maybe we didn't get off on the best foot," she said to Stephanie. "So, I was thinking, maybe tonight after work, we hang out and have a few drinks and get to know each other."

She looked at them looking at each other.

"Sounds good to me," Dillon said. "Stephanie?"

"Sure. What have I got to lose?"

"Most excellent," Dillon said. "I think this was a great idea, Leah."

"Thanks," Leah said. "Anything to clear the air."

At the end of the day, they grabbed a table and Dillon went to the bar to get their first round.

"Are you nervous?" Leah said to Stephanie. "You seem nervous."

"Maybe a little. I'm worried now that you're taking the time to get to know me that you won't like me."

"Dillon seems to think you're wonderful. She's rarely wrong."

Dillon was back then with their drinks.

"Here's to the three musketeers," she said.

"Here's to a civil working arrangement," Stephanie said.

"Here's to a fun work environment," Leah said.

They clinked their glasses together and each took a sip. Leah's dirty martini was perfect.

"This is so good."

"Thank you," Dillon said.

"Did you go back there and make it yourself?"

"I did. Only the first one because I wanted it to be perfect. The next one we'll have to trust the bartenders."

"Sounds good."

They had a few drinks and soon Leah was feeling no pain.

"I think we need food," she said. "At least I know I do."

"Mexican sounds delicious," Dillon said.

"Ooh, yeah."

"Actually," Stephanie said. "I think I'll head on home. I've got food to eat there and I'm ready for some quiet time."

MJ WILLIAMZ

"Are you sure?" Leah said. "We're buying."

"Thanks, but no thanks. I've had enough to drink and like I said, I have food at home. I'll see you two in the morning."

Leah watched her walk off.

"Was it something I said?"

"I don't think so. I think she was having as much fun as we were."

"Okay. Well, I was enjoying her. I have to admit it. I was looking forward to getting to know her even better over dinner."

"I think you were successful in breaking the ice, don't you?"

"I do. And I have to admit, I really like her. I mean, if you have to be sleeping with someone, I guess I understand why you chose her."

Dillon couldn't believe her ears. If she had to be sleeping with somebody? Like she should remain celibate while Leah slept around? It wasn't fair. She knew it, but Leah apparently still hadn't caught on.

"Are you okay to drive?" she said.

"Probably not. Are you?"

"Yeah. I'm fine. Let's go get some food in you."

They drove to Leah's favorite restaurant where Leah ordered a margarita, but Dillon stuck with beer. They laughed and joked and talked about the years they'd known each other.

"Do you remember the night we met?" Dillon said.

"Sure. We closed down the old lesbian bar, then went to have coffee at the Diner. I remember it was pouring down rain and you gave me your umbrella. I thought you were such a gentlebutch."

Dillon had to fight to keep from telling her she'd wanted her since that very night. It would have been so easy to say something, but she kept it to herself. Just as she had all these years since. It was shortly after their meeting that Dillon had introduced Leah to Sueann, something she'd regretted from the beginning.

After they'd eaten and Leah had had two margaritas, Leah's eyes had a glazed look to them, and Dillon knew she was pretty toasty.

"Let's get you back to my place," she said. "You can crash there tonight."

In the truck, Leah reached over and took Dillon's hand.

"What would I do without you?" she said.

Every muscle in Dillon's body tensed at the contact. She loved it and wished Leah would never let go.

"You'll never have to worry about that," she said.

"Will you make me another dirty martini?" Leah asked when they got to Dillon's house.

"Are you sure? I'd hate for you to get sick."

"I'm fine. One more drink. Then come join me on the couch, okay?"

Dillon mixed a drink for Leah and grabbed a beer for herself. She walked back out to the couch and sat next to Leah. She was close enough to breathe the soft scent of her perfume and feel her body heat radiating off of her. It was pure torture, but she couldn't resist.

Leah took a sip of her drink and set her glass down. She moved closer to Dillon.

"You know what I was thinking?"

Dillon swallowed hard.

"What's that?"

"I could show you what I've learned so far."

Dillon's heart raced.

"What do you mean?"

"You're gorgeous, Dillon. I've always found you attractive."

The words went straight to Dillon's clit.

"And I was thinking it might be fun for the two of us to mess around. I have no doubt you know what you're doing in bed and I'd love to show you all I've learned. I think you'd enjoy it."

She leaned in and kissed Dillon softly. Every one of Dillon's nerves was taut with need. Leah was actually offering herself to her. She could finally have her. But Leah was drunk, and Dillon refused to take advantage of her.

"Maybe some other time," she said.

Leah pouted.

"Don't you find me attractive?"

"Very much, Leah. But I think I'd rather you be sober if we're ever going to make love."

"I'm sober enough."

Dillon shook her head.

"I don't think so. I tell you what. If you remember this in the morning and want to talk about it then, we can. For now, I think we need to get you to bed. Alone."

"Won't you at least hold me?"

"I don't think that's a good idea either."

"You're being a party pooper."

"I'm being rational. Come on, now. Let's get you in bed."

She helped Leah walk down the hall to her room. Leah started to undress while Dillon was still in the room. She bid her a hasty good night and closed the door behind her. In the living room, Dillon pulled a cover over her as she lay on the couch fighting the urge to touch herself. She was so worked up and needed relief. But maybe Leah would remember this in the morning, and maybe something could finally happen between them.

CHAPTER SEVENTEEN

L eah woke the next morning, disoriented and with a throbbing headache. She slowly came to realize she was in Dillon's bed. But where was Dillon? Oh, yeah. The previous night's conversation came back to her. She'd asked Dillon to go to bed with her, but Dillon had declined. So now she was embarrassed as well as hung over. She pulled her clothes on and followed the smell of coffee.

"Hey," she said when she saw Dillon at her kitchen table sipping coffee. Her wet hair was slicked back and she smelled of soap and shampoo. She looked more handsome than Leah had ever seen her. Was she really attracted to Dillon? Like, that way? Why had that never occurred to her before?

"Hey," Dillon said. "How are you this morning?"

"My head hurts and I'm embarrassed."

"I've got ibuprofen for the headache. As for the embarrassment, you've got nothing to be embarrassed about."

"Are you serious? I threw myself at you last night."

"And?"

"And you clearly weren't interested. So now I'm embarrassed."

She took the ibuprofen Dillon handed her. When their hands met, she felt chills cover her body.

"Do you remember the whole conversation?"

"No. Just have a vague recollection that I begged you to come to bed with me. And you refused."

"And why did I refuse?"

"You weren't interested."

"No. You were too drunk."

"No? You mean you'd actually sleep with me?"

"Would you actually sleep with me? I think that's more the question," Dillon said.

"Can we let Stephanie open the bar and go get grease for breakfast?"

She wasn't trying to change the subject, but saw from the look in Dillon's eyes that that's how it came across. She just thought she'd be able to think more clearly after she got some food in her system.

Dillon texted Stephanie. She got her answer and looked up from her phone.

"Stephanie's fine with that. Now why don't you go shower? I think you'll feel better."

For some reason, Leah really wanted to invite Dillon to join her, but thought better. What was going on? When had she become obsessed with her best friend? It was odd, but it was real. There was no denying how she was feeling. But what would it be like? A one-night stand? A relationship? No. She shook her head. She was getting way ahead of herself. She needed food and coffee and then she'd be able to make rational decisions.

Dillon was waiting on the couch when Leah came out of the bedroom wearing the same clothes she'd had on the day before.

"Do you mind if we swing by my place so I can put on clean clothes?"

"I don't mind at all."

Once Leah was ready, they headed for the Diner and ordered greasy breakfasts and lots of coffee. Leah was already starting to feel better. But was she thinking any more clearly? That was the question. Dillon was awfully quiet, which made Leah nervous.

"Penny for your thoughts," she said.

"Just waiting for you to feel better," Dillon said.

"I feel much better. Thanks. This is just what I needed."

"Good. I'm glad."

"So what are your thoughts on last night?" Leah said apprehensively.

"I think your thoughts are more important."

"How do you figure?"

"You're the one that started the conversation. I need to know if it was just drunk ramblings or if you were serious."

Leah was silent. Why wouldn't Dillon throw her a bone?

Her phone pinged. She checked it. It was a woman named Chandra asking for a date. She looked at it but didn't respond.

"Who's that?" Dillon said.

"Someone asking for a date."

"Ah. Well, I guess that answers my question about whether or not you were serious last night."

"Huh? Why?"

"I don't know. Look, let's get going. We need to do some work before the lunch rush."

"No. I want to know why you said that."

"I don't know that I just want to be another notch in your belt, Leah. Another experiment for you to try. I just don't think that's what I want."

"And you think that's what I want?"

"Whatever. Just answer your date."

They drove back to the bar in silence. When they arrived, they said hello to Stephanie. Dillon stayed behind the bar, but Leah went into the office. She didn't have time to enter her accounting. She had to go buy meats and produce for the lunch rush. She was glad to get away from Dillon. She was so embarrassed by what had happened the night before, yet Dillon had seemed to be open to the idea of sleeping together.

What did Leah want? That was the question. Her phone pinged again. It was Chandra again asking if they could meet that night. Leah responded that she'd be happy to meet her at the bar at six. She didn't want to drink, that was for sure, but she could wait there until Chandra arrived.

Leah finished her errands and barricaded herself in the office until it was time for her shift. She walked out behind the bar.

"Thanks for last night," Stephanie said. "I had a really good time.

"Thanks. Me, too."

"I think we should do it again sometime."

"That sounds great."

Dillon came out of the kitchen with a burger. Leah knew she needed to ask her to stay at the bar that night, but wasn't sure how to go about doing it.

"So I have a favor to ask," Leah said.

"What's that?"

"I have a date tonight."

"Of course you do."

"Dillon..."

"What?"

"Nothing. Anyway, would you mind meeting her with me?"

"What time?"

"Six?"

"Fine," Dillon said. "I'll be here."

Six o'clock rolled around and Chandra showed up right on time. Dillon sat like a rock, barely talking to Leah. But she shook hands with Chandra before excusing herself.

"Your best friend doesn't seem very nice," Chandra said.

"She's in a bad mood. She had a rough night last night."

"Bummer for her. Let's get out of here."

After dinner, Chandra and Leah drove to Leah's house. Once inside, Chandra kissed Leah hard. She slid her tongue inside Leah's mouth, and Leah allowed herself to be kissed passionately. She tried to return the feelings, but Dillon was in the back of her mind. When Chandra moved her hand over Leah's breast, Leah pulled away.

"I can't do this. I'm sorry, but I can't."

"What are you talking about? This is the deal. This is what your profile says you want." She kissed her again.

Leah pulled away.

"I know what my profile says. But I just can't do it tonight. I'm really sorry."

"You're a fuckin' tease. And a bitch."

She slammed the door behind her. Leah grabbed her phone and deleted her profile. She was done.

Leah got to work late the next morning. She walked in to find Dillon working on her laptop.

"I quit," Leah said.

Dillon looked up.

"What? You can't quit. We own this place together. Do you want me to buy you out? Because I'm not sure I could afford that."

Leah smiled.

"That's not what I meant. I meant I quit Girl World. I'm tired of having sex with strangers. They don't mean anything and I'm starting to feel cheap and sleazy."

Starting to? Dillon was glad she'd finally come to that conclusion. There was still the unresolved subject of them, but this was definitely a step in the right direction.

"Don't you have anything to say about it?" Leah said.

"Yeah. I think if you feel the time is right, then it's the right thing to do."

"It started out as a good thing. You know. I had a lot to learn. But now, the encounters just feel empty to me, you know?"

"So last night didn't go so well, I take it?"

"No. I kicked her out before we got into it. She called me a tease and a bitch."

"I'm sorry."

And she really was sorry. It pissed her off to think of anyone talking to Leah like that. She was too nice of a person to be called those things.

"Thanks," Leah said. "But I guess I deserved it."

"I don't know about that."

"My profile pretty much said I was going to put out, so when I didn't, I deserved to be told off."

"Still, I don't think it was very nice of her."

"Thanks. You're always looking out for me."

"And I always will," Dillon said.

They sat in silence for a moment.

"Well, I guess I'd better hit the books," Leah said.

"Yeah, and I'll go see if Stephanie needs any help setting up." Dillon was all smiles as she exited the office. Leah had finally given up her app dating, and Dillon had to hope that boded well for her. She wondered how to proceed now. Leah hadn't said she didn't want to sleep with her, but Dillon wanted more and Leah hadn't agreed to that. But maybe now that she wasn't sleeping around with every Jane in town, she'd realize Dillon had been there all along.

"You're in a good mood," Stephanie said.

"I am."

"And it's not my fault because I was alone in my bed last night."

"Right. Sorry about that. I should have come over, but I wasn't in a very good mood yesterday."

"I noticed. It doesn't take a rocket scientist to read your moods, Dillon."

"No. I suppose it doesn't."

"So why the smiles today?"

"Life's just good, Stephanie. Life's just good."

The morning crowd of regulars shuffled in, and Stephanie served them and flirted with them. Dillon leaned on the bar and visited with them until Leah came out of the office.

"I'm off to run errands," she said.

"See you soon," Dillon said. And she couldn't wait. She was excited for Leah to get back. Maybe she'd broach the subject of them again.

Leah returned and disappeared into the office to work during the lunch rush. When it was over, she came out and relieved Dillon for a while. She and Stephanie finally looked coordinated behind the bar. This made Dillon happy. They finally got along. Would that continue if she quit sleeping with Stephanie?

Her life had gotten so complicated lately. It used to be so simple. No attachments anywhere and love Leah from afar. Now, she was sleeping with a bartender. Was that an attachment? She certainly didn't think so, but wasn't sure Stephanie felt that way. And now she had to wonder if she could let her feelings for Leah show. How would Stephanie take that? How would Leah?

She almost wished she could go back to the way it was. But she was so close with Leah. Would she really rather not be? It was torture this way, but it had been the other way as well. She took another bite of burger. Yeah. Life was complicated.

It was her turn behind the bar. Leah sat down on the other side of the bar and ordered a drink.

"Are you sure?" Dillon said.

"Sure. Why not?"

"Okay. One dirty martini coming up."

"You want me to make it?" Stephanie said.

"No. I got it. I know just how she likes it."

She mixed the drink and went to set it on the bar. Leah took it from her hand instead. Their fingers touched for just a millisecond too long. Their gazes met, and Dillon coughed as she looked away. She looked over to gratefully see Stephanie busy with other customers. She had things under control, so Dillon just leaned on the bar talking to Leah. She looked so damned cute that day. She was in serious need of a haircut, so she had her hair pulled back in a ponytail. Dillon wanted desperately to kiss and nuzzle her neck and see if she liked it. She realized she had no idea what Leah liked. While many women from Girl World, strangers all of them, knew just how to make her feel good, Dillon did not. But she'd certainly give it her best shot if given the opportunity.

"So are you finished for the day?" Dillon said.

"I think so. I don't want to do anything else."

"Does that mean you're going to sit here and get drunk?"

Leah laughed.

"No. Definitely not getting drunk. Just having a drink."

"Sounds good."

"Join me?"

Dillon looked around. Stephanie definitely had things under control, and Dillon could always go back behind the bar if needed. She popped the top off a beer and joined Leah.

"Stephanie really is a good worker," Leah said.

"Yep."

"I'm sorry I gave you such a hard time."

"No worries. It's all good."

"I was wondering. Would you like to go to dinner tonight?"

"What's the occasion tonight?"

"Do we need an occasion?" Leah said.

"No. I guess we don't."

"We can drop my car off at my house and you can drive. If that's okay."

"Sounds good to me. What are you in the mood for?"

"Steak and lobster."

"Wow. Okay then. We know where we'll be going."

The place got busy and Leah and Dillon both ended up behind the bar helping Stephanie. They worked well together and soon their shift was over.

"You guys want to hang out and have a few?" Stephanie said.

"No thanks," Leah said. "I think I'm up for a quiet night."

That was odd. Why hadn't she told her they were going out for dinner? She must have a reason.

"Yeah. I'm ready to get out of here, too. I'll see you tomorrow."

Dillon drove over to Leah's and got there before her. She waited in her truck until Leah pulled in her drive. Leah walked over to the driver's window.

"You want to come in for a beer first?"

Dillon got butterflies in her stomach. She'd been in Leah's house many, many times, but somehow something felt different.

"Sure."

She got out of her truck and followed Leah inside. She took the beer and sat on the couch. Leah sat next to her.

"I just kind of wanted to unwind a little before we head out," Leah said.

"No problem. I'll never turn down a free beer."

"Good."

They finished their drinks and headed to the restaurant. It was the middle of the week, so the place was fairly empty. They were seated quickly and Dillon ordered a bottle of wine for them.

"So seriously," she said. "To what do I owe this pleasure?"

"Can't a girl want to go out with a handsome woman without a reason?"

Handsome, huh?

"I suppose she can," Dillon said. She raised her glass. "To us."

Leah hesitated only briefly before she replied.

"To us."

They clinked their glasses and each took a sip.

"I do love Malbec," Leah said.

"As do I."

Their dinner came and they kept the conversation light, but Dillon swore Leah was being somewhat flirtatious. More than somewhat, actually. And she had Dillon feeling all kinds of things she'd kept tamped down for so many years. She felt like maybe she had a chance. Maybe. Just maybe.

When they left the restaurant, Leah took Dillon's hand as they walked through the parking lot. Leah's hand was soft and smooth and warm. Just as Dillon knew her whole body would be. Even parts she scarcely let herself think about.

She stopped and looked at Leah.

"What are you doing?"

"Nothing."

She said it in a singsong voice and smiled coquettishly. Dillon felt the fire inside her burn hotter.

They drove back to Leah's.

"Would you like to come in for a beer before you head home?"
Dillon hesitated.

"What happened to 'I never turn down a free beer'?"
Dillon smiled.

"Okay. Okay. Just one won't hurt."

She followed Leah inside. Leah turned on some music and dimmed the lights before she sat down with Dillon on the couch.

"What is this?" Dillon said. "Setting the mood?"

"Something like that."

"Are you trying to seduce me?"

"I honestly don't know. Maybe."

Dillon looked into her eyes. They weren't glazed. Still, she had to ask.

"Are you drunk?"

"No. I'm not drunk."

"What do you want from me, Leah? Please tell me."

"I want you to kiss me."

"Why?"

"What? Never mind." She stood. "Maybe this wasn't such a good idea."

Dillon took her hand and gently pulled her back down.

"Please. Don't be upset. I just need to know what you want."

"I don't know. I honestly don't know. I only know I really want you to kiss me. When I kissed you the other night, something felt right about it. I think I've been a fool all this time. I think what I want, or who I want, has been right before my eyes."

"I'd like to believe that, Leah. I really would."

She hadn't released Leah's hand. She held it in her lap. She used it to pull Leah closer. She leaned in slowly and watched as Leah's eyes closed and her lips parted. She lowered her mouth to them and closed hers over Leah's. Leah's lips were so soft and Dillon wanted more.

Dillon stood.

"I think I'd better go."

"What? Why?"

"Because I really like you, Leah. I always have. And I really like kissing you. But I'm afraid it's going to lead to something I'm not sure you're ready for."

"I'm ready. Oh, dear God, Dillon. I'm ready."

"You're ready for a roll in the hay. Sure. But are you ready for more? Only you can answer that. And I'll wait for your answer."

She drove home a hormonal mess.

CHAPTER EIGHTEEN

Leah pulled into the parking lot the next morning at work. She saw that Dillon's truck was already there as well as Stephanie's car. Her heart skipped a beat when she saw Dillon's truck. She couldn't explain why she was suddenly so into her. It explained her reaction to her sleeping with Stephanie, though. She was jealous. Pure and simple. Dillon had been the one all along.

She thought of their kiss the night before. It was soft and sweet, but it had left her craving so much more. She had a need only Dillon could satiate. But why did Dillon leave? And what would it be like seeing her in the office? She took a deep breath to steel herself and got out of her car.

Stephanie was setting up the bar when she walked in.

"Good morning, Leah," she said pleasantly.

Leah tried to calm her nerves and made herself smile.

"Good morning. How are you?"

"Great. And you?"

"Not bad. Thanks."

She braced herself and opened the office door. Dillon looked up from her laptop. Leah let the door close behind her, but stayed standing. Dillon turned in her chair.

"What's up?"

"You tell me."

"You okay?"

"Are you? Are we?" Leah said.

"I'm great," Dillon said. "As for us, that's entirely up to you."

"Last night was nice."

"Yes, it was."

"I definitely wanted more."

"Ah, yes. But how much more?"

"I don't know."

Leah sat in her chair.

"I realize now that the reason I freaked over you and Stephanie was because I was jealous."

Dillon arched an eyebrow at her.

"Really?"

"Really," Leah said.

"How so?"

"I wanted to be the one you were with. Not her."

"Well, now you know how I feel. I'd love to be with you. But not just for a night or two. I want a long-term commitment."

"But it's so soon after Sueann. I'm afraid to get into a long-term relationship again."

"Okay," Dillon said. "That makes sense. You're more into one-night stands right now. And I'm not going to be one. So here's where we have our impasse."

"But I'm tired of one-night stands. I'm tired of meaningless sex."

"So, where does that leave us?"

"I'm scared, Dillon. I'm so scared."

"Fine then," Dillon said softly. "We can take things slow. Dates, kissing. Just like last night until you're no longer afraid."

"But would you be okay with that? I mean would that be enough for you?"

"Leah, I've waited this long for you. What's a little while longer?"

"Can I ask you a question?" Leah said.

"Sure. Go for it."

"How long have you wanted me?"

Dillon laughed. It wasn't a mocking laugh. It was a genuine laugh.

"From the moment I first laid eyes on you, Leah. From the very beginning."

"Wow. And you never said anything?"

"I wanted to that very first night. But you were kind of drunk and I didn't want to take advantage of you."

Leah stared at Dillon. She was so touched by the kindness inside her handsome shell. Leah could do a lot worse. She knew that. Her heart had started doing somersaults at just the thought of Dillon lately. Why couldn't she put her fear aside and give Dillon a shot?

She and Dillon both checked the clock on the wall.

"Well," Dillon said. "It's time for me to go to work. Would you like to go out again tonight?"

"Yes. I would. I'd like that very much."

"Great."

She watched Dillon walk out of the office and pondered her moves for the night. She really wanted Dillon. No, she needed her. With every ounce of her being, she needed Dillon to take her. Just being around her that morning had her insides buzzing and her underwear damp. She was a mess. One hot mess. And Dillon Franklin was the only one who could offer her relief.

Alone in the office, she tried to remember their first meeting. She remembered closing down the old lesbian bar with Dillon. She had just met her that night. They went for coffee afterward. Dillon had seemed so out of her reach. She was kind and funny and sexy as hell, but Leah thought Dillon was just being nice to her. She had no idea Dillon had been interested. Was it really possible that they could have been together this whole time? She shook her head. These thoughts weren't doing her any good. It was shortly after that that Dillon had introduced her to Sueann, and the rest, as they say, was history.

She forced herself to focus on her bookkeeping and when she was ready to run errands, she left the office and watched Dillon and Stephanie laughing and joking behind the bar. She felt the old jealousy rear its ugly head, but she told herself to be calm. It was her that Dillon wanted. Not Stephanie. They could tease and flirt as much as they wanted. She was the one who would end up with Dillon. As soon as the terror subsided.

"The other boss lady seems to be in a good mood today," Stephanie said.

"That she is. And that's a good thing. She deserves a little happiness, too," Dillon said.

"But she's been dating so many women. How is it none of them stole her heart? Or has one done that now?"

"I told you before, her dating isn't something I'm comfortable talking about. If you want to know more about it, you'll have to ask her."

Deep inside, Dillon hoped she wouldn't ask Leah. Then Leah might say something about Dillon and her. And Dillon felt she should be the one to tell Stephanie about them. If there was a them. Or ever would be.

The bar was open for business and Martha wandered up to the bar. She ordered her drink, and while Stephanie mixed it, started on the two of them again.

"When are you two going to start dating?" she said. "You'd make a fine couple."

"She's my employee," Dillon said. She was smiling. Martha gave them crap about dating on a regular basis. But this time, she caught Dillon off guard.

"What about you and Leah then? Talk about a great looking couple. You're already a power couple in business. Why not be one socially as well?"

Stephanie laughed, but Dillon choked. She sputtered, trying to sound coherent, but failing miserably.

"I, um, that is, Leah's off the market right now," she said.

"Ah, but you'd date her if she wasn't?" Stephanie said.

Dillon looked over at her and couldn't read her expression. Was she playing or accusing?

"That's not what I said."

"But you're not denying it either."

Stephanie went to the other end of the bar to help another customer. Dillon leaned over the bar and whispered at Martha.

"Troublemaker."

Martha cackled.

"I'm just funnin' you, you know. Gotta have something to do to keep myself entertained. How was I to know I was hitting too close to home?"

Dillon chose not to reply but then realized Stephanie had joined them.

"Not too close for me," Stephanie said. "I can't speak for Dillon."

Dillon went back into the office to calm down. She knew she had to have a talk with Stephanie; she just didn't want to do it in front of patrons, least of all nosy Martha. Yes, she would date Leah in a heartbeat. And she was sort of dating her now, right? Just because they weren't sleeping together. Yet. She shook her head. She couldn't wait for the lunch rush. She needed to be busy so she could quit thinking.

Leah came back from her errands to find her in the office.

"What's going on? Why aren't you behind the bar?" she said.

"Stephanie seemed to have a grip."

"Well, it's picking up now."

There was a knock on the door and Stephanie opened it slightly.

"A little help out here?"

Dillon got up and went out to help with the craziness that was lunch. The next two hours passed with little to do but wait on customers and clean up after them. She was actually sad when the rush slowed to a steady stream. She continued to help, and soon Leah joined them.

The three of them worked until things slowed down enough for Dillon to go back into the office. She updated their social media pages and looked over prices of new felt for the pool tables. She finally had nothing to do and no reason to hide in there any longer. She went into the kitchen to make a burger. Leah joined her.

"You okay?" she said.

"Sure. Why?"

"You just seemed to be in the office for a while. I want to make sure you're not avoiding me."

"Avoiding you? Hell, no. And we're going out tonight, right? So why would I avoid you?"

"Are you avoiding Stephanie, then?"

"No. Maybe. I don't know."

"We can talk about this tonight, if you'd like."

"That sounds good," Dillon said.

Leah went back to the bar and Dillon finished making her lunch. She sat at the bar and ate as she tried to ignore Stephanie and Leah. When she was through, she went back behind the bar and Leah went back to the office. Happy hour kept the place jumping. When their shift had ended, Stephanie poured herself a glass of wine and sat on the other side of the bar.

"Anyone want to join me?" she said.

Dillon looked to Leah, who shrugged.

"Sure," Dillon said. "I'll have a beer."

"I'll join you, too," Leah said.

Dillon breathed a sigh of relief. She really hadn't wanted to sit alone with Stephanie. She knew she was avoiding her, but couldn't help it. It wasn't that she wasn't sure she needed to cut the cord with her. It was more she wasn't sure how she would react to her dating Leah.

They finished their drinks and Dillon said good night. She drove to Leah's house and let herself in. She grabbed a beer from the refrigerator and made herself comfortable on the couch. Soon, she heard Leah come in.

"Dillon?"

"In here."

Leah appeared in the doorway looking gorgeous. At the bar, she was beautiful. There was no denying that. But get her out of that element and seeing her in her own home, she was just stunning.

"You look amazing," Dillon said.

"I'm wearing the same thing I've been wearing all day."

"But you look gorgeous now. Out of the bar, there's just more to your beauty."

Leah blushed.

"Well, thank you. Are you ready to get going?"

Dillon held up her beer.

"I just opened this. You want me to mix you a drink?"

"No, thanks. I'll just sit here and relax, if that's okay."

"Sure."

Dillon patted the couch next to her.

Leah sat.

"So..."

"Yeah?" Dillon said. Her chest tightened. Was Leah going to answer her finally? Was she going to tell her she was ready for a commitment?

"About Stephanie."

"Ah. Yeah. What about her?"

"Have you broken things off with her?"

"No. But I haven't slept with her in a while. There's really nothing to break off. We were just having casual sex."

"But you haven't told her you won't sleep with her anymore." It was a statement, not a question.

"And you?" Dillon said. "Have you decided on what you want from me?"

"So is this the chicken and the egg gig? You won't tell her until I've made a commitment to you? And I don't know I can make a commitment to you with her still in the picture."

Dillon sat silently sipping her beer. If she was dating Leah, she would do so exclusively. Even if they hadn't agreed on a long-term goal yet. She knew she had finally found happiness with Leah, the happiness she'd fantasized about for so long. She didn't need Stephanie.

"I have no problem telling Stephanie I won't see her anymore," she finally said.

"Good. That would make me happy."

She moved closer to Dillon, who kissed her on top of her head.

"That's all I want. To make you happy."

"Then stay the night tonight."

"Nope. I'm not going to do that."

"Please, Dillon. I need you."

Leah knelt on the couch and pressed her lips to Dillon's. Dillon felt the heat wash over her body. She wrapped her free arm around Leah and pulled her close. She felt her pressed into her as their kiss deepened. Dillon used every ounce of self-control to end the kiss.

"We should get to dinner," she said.

"Your voice is hoarse. You can't deny the effect I have on you."

"I don't try to deny it, kiddo. I want you with every bit of my being. But I can wait until you're ready. I want you, but I don't want to be another experiment for you. I don't want you using me to practice on. I want it to be real and permanent."

"Okay. You're right. We should go to dinner."

On the way, Leah took Dillon's hand in hers. She looked over at Dillon and questioned yet again why she was so hesitant to commit. Dillon was by far the most attractive woman Leah had ever met. And she was caring and compassionate. And the best friend Leah had ever had.

Fuck Sueann for making her gun-shy to get into another relationship. But Dillon wasn't Sueann, she reminded herself. Far from it.

They went for Thai food. It was a place Leah had never been and she happily let Dillon order for her. Dillon knew what she liked. Dillon knew everything about her. All her secrets and fears. Everything. She was an open book to Dillon. And she wanted to open up other parts to her as well. But was the chance of getting hurt worth it?

"You're going to love the food," Dillon said. "It's light and flavorful, but it'll fill you up."

"I'm loving this Thai tea. It's delicious."

"Excellent."

And then they sat in silence. That had never happened before. They always had something to talk about. But Leah knew Dillon was waiting on her to make up her mind, but she couldn't do it. Not yet.

"I blame Sueann," Leah said finally.

"Huh?"

"She hurt me real bad, Dillon."

"I know."

"And now I'm scared to try again." There. She'd said it.

"I'm willing to take this as slow as we need to. Just know, I'm not going to sleep with you until you're ready."

"I am ready."

"You know what I mean."

Leah sat back against her chair. She looked at Dillon. She didn't look mad or upset in any way. She was just being honest. Leah felt the burning behind her eyes. What the fuck? She wasn't going to cry. There was nothing to cry about. Or was there? Dillon was so patient and she felt so bad for making her wait.

"I know what you mean. I just don't want to make another mistake," Leah said.

"I'm not Sueann."

"Oh, God. Don't I know that."

"Good. Keep that in mind. And, please, don't compare us."

Leah knew she'd been doing just that.

After dinner, they drove back to Leah's house.

"Would you like to come in?"

"I'd love to, but I think I'd better not."

"Okay. Well, thanks for dinner."

"You're welcome."

Leah leaned over and kissed Dillon's cheek. Her strong jaw flexed. She knew she was making this hard on both of them.

Once alone in her house, Leah sat on the couch and put her face in her hands. She had anybody's dream woman after her and she was too afraid to say okay. Why hadn't Dillon wanted to come in? Was she off to Stephanie's now? She couldn't stand the thought of it.

Her mind kept going to Dillon's strong profile as they drove home. And her dark, penetrating eyes as she watched her try the different foods at the restaurant. She was definitely the most handsome woman she'd ever met, she thought for the millionth time.

She walked back to her room, dropping her clothes as she went. She was naked by the time she got to her bed, and she climbed up and ran her hands all over her body. She closed her eyes. In her mind's eyes, they were Dillon's large, strong, capable hands.

It was those hands that slid between her legs. She was wet and ready and slipped her fingers inside. She felt so good. Next, she slid them over her slick, swollen clit and brought herself to three powerful orgasms.

CHAPTER NINETEEN

Dillon climbed into bed after her date. Her heart raced and her body throbbed with the denial she was forcing on herself. Finally, finally, Leah was ready to offer her body to Dillon, and she wasn't ready to accept it. She felt like a fool, but knew what she wanted and was going to be patient enough to get it. Her phone buzzed. She checked it. Stephanie.

You wanna come over?
It's late. I'm already in bed.
So when are we gonna talk?
About?
Leah.
There's nothing to talk about.
Whatever.
I'll see you tomorrow.
Good night"

She set her phone back on her nightstand and closed her eyes. Sleep escaped her. Her stomach was filled with dread over her upcoming talk with Stephanie. She knew it was necessary, and she hoped Stephanie would be okay with it. She just wished she'd told her before Martha forced Dillon's hand. Oh well. Nothing she could do about it now.

She finally fell into a restless sleep and woke up tired and cranky. She made herself coffee and stood under the hot water in her shower for a long time. Her muscles finally relaxed and she sipped some coffee while she dressed. When she was ready to leave, she ran some gel through her hair and headed out the door.

Stephanie's car was in the parking lot already. Either she'd gotten there early or she'd left it there the night before. Either way, it just reminded Dillon of the talk she had to have with her. She braced herself as she checked to see if the back door was unlocked, but it wasn't. Stephanie must have left her car there the night before.

Dillon went to the office and started her work when there was a knock on the door and Stephanie walked in.

"Sorry about texting you so late last night," she said. "I was pretty lit."

Dillon laughed.

"Haven't we all done something like that before? No worries." She took a deep breath. "But as long as you're here, have a seat."

"Before you say anything, Dillon, we weren't an item. You don't have to break up with me."

"And I appreciate that. But I do need to let you know I won't be sleeping with you anymore."

"And I suppose Leah fits into this somewhere?" Stephanie said.

"Yes. Yes, she does. We're going to try dating."

"Good for you. Like I said before, you've obviously had feelings for each other for a long time. I'm glad you're finally acting on them."

"Thanks for being so understanding."

"No problem." She stood. "And, Dillon? Thanks for all the good times."

"Thank you."

Stephanie left the office just as Leah was walking in.

"What was that about?" Leah said.

"I just told her you and I were dating and I wouldn't be sleeping with her anymore."

"Wow."

"Wow? That's it? Wow?"

"I guess I'm just surprised. I mean, not so much that you told her you wouldn't sleep with her, but that you and I are dating."

"Well, we are, aren't we?" Dillon said.

"Yes."

"Okay, so why not tell her?"

Leah sat down.

"I don't know. It's just that that makes it so...official, I guess."

"Are you embarrassed to be dating me?"

"No. Not at all."

"Okay, so it's no biggie."

"You're right. And thank you. For doing that, I mean."

"You're welcome."

Dillon went out behind the bar to help Stephanie and see how she was really doing.

"So, you're sure we're okay?" she said.

"Oh, yeah, we're fine. I'm honestly very happy for you. Both of you."

"Thanks."

They opened the bar and Leah took off to run her errands.

"I do have to ask you a question, though," Stephanie said.

"Shoot."

"How do you feel about the fact that she was sleeping with all those women? I mean, that can't sit well with you."

"There was a reason for what she was doing. And who said she was sleeping with them all?"

Stephanie shrugged.

"Just a hunch."

"Well, you don't know what she was doing, so don't concern yourself with it, okay?"

"Suit yourself. I just know it would bug me. I'd feel like I was getting sloppy seconds or something."

"Is this your passive-aggressive side?" Dillon said. "Because it's not very attractive."

"No. I'm sorry. I'm fine. Really. I just wondered. But you're right. It's none of my business."

Leah came back with the groceries, and Dillon and Stephanie powered through the lunch rush. Then Dillon disappeared into the office and Leah came out to work with Stephanie.

"So, I don't think I ever officially apologized for freaking out that night," Leah said.

"What night?"

"The night I saw you and Dillon making out in the parking lot."

"Oh. Don't worry about it. I have to admit, I wondered at the time if there were some latent emotions going on there."

"You did, did you? Even I hadn't considered that."

"Ah, but you have now, haven't you?"

"Yep. And I know now I was just jealous."

"Well, I'm honestly happy for the two of you," Stephanie said.

"Thank you."

The afternoon was slow, and Leah fought to make herself stay out there with Stephanie. She kept trying to think of a reason to go back into the office and spend some time with Dillon. She was just about ready to go in there when a crowd of people walked in and she and Stephanie had to ask Dillon to come out and help them.

The three of them worked hard trying to keep up with the orders and bussing the tables. The crowd left just as happy hour began and it was crazy for another two hours. Finally, their shift came to an end and they sat on the other side of the bar sipping their drinks.

"Wow, what a day," Stephanie said.

"It was nutso," Dillon said. "But it'll sure look good when Leah does the books tomorrow."

"Yes, it will," Leah said.

They finished their drinks and Leah stood.

"Would you like to join us for dinner, Stephanie?" she said.

"I'd hate to be the third wheel."

"No. You won't. It'll be a business dinner, anyway."

"Sure then. I'll join you."

"We'll meet you at the usual Mexican place. I'm going to drive home and have Dillon give me a ride."

"Sounds good."

Leah parked her car and climbed into Dillon's truck. She kissed her on the cheek.

"So, what's with inviting Stephanie to dinner?" Dillon said.

"I'm going to give her a raise."

Dillon raised her eyebrows.

"Are you doing it out of guilt?"

"No. I'm doing it because we can afford it and that woman works her ass off for us."

"Well, I think it's great. And it might ensure she stays around."

"That's what I'm hoping."

They got to the restaurant to find Stephanie already at a table sipping a margarita. She waved them over.

"Hey there. Hope you don't mind. I got started without you."

Leah laughed.

"Not a problem. That looks good. I think I'll have the same."

Dillon stuck with beer, and once they had their drinks and had placed their orders, Leah looked at Stephanie.

"So, I told you this was a business dinner."

"Yeah. Is everything okay?"

"Everything is better than okay. I'd, that is, we'd like to give you a raise."

"Seriously?" Stephanie broke into a wide smile. Her whole face lit up. "I mean, are you sure?"

"Positive," Leah said. She was happy to see the joy on Stephanie's face. "You work so hard, you deserve another three dollars an hour."

"Oh, my God. That's a lot of money," Stephanie said.

"You deserve it," Dillon said.

"Wow. Well, thank you both so much. You know how much I love my job. I almost feel like I'd be willing to do it for free. But then there's those pesky bills and all."

They all laughed. Leah relaxed and took a sip of her drink. She was confident Stephanie wouldn't move on now. At least not any time soon. And they needed her. She was a wonderful employee.

After dinner, they said their good-byes in the parking lot. Stephanie hugged Dillon first and Leah felt a twinge of jealousy. She hugged Leah next and Leah realized she was just being ridiculous.

"Thank you both again. So much."

"Thank you, Stephanie," Leah said.

"I'll see you guys in the morning."

"Good night," Dillon said.

As soon as they were in Dillon's truck, Leah took her hand and rested their interlocked hands together on her thigh. She grew hot at the feeling. She needed Dillon so badly and wondered if that night would be the night.

They arrived back at her house and she invited Dillon in for a beer. Dillon seemed to hesitate.

"I promise not to jump your bones," Leah said. "It won't be easy, but I promise."

Dillon laughed.

"I suppose one beer won't hurt."

They sat on the couch and Leah searched her brain for the best way to broach a subject that had driven her mad since the day they'd met.

"So, tell me about your childhood," she said.

"Not much to tell."

"Aw, come on. I know Franklin isn't your real last name."

"Sure it is. It's legal and everything."

"Okay, but it's not your birth name. With your olive skin, dark hair and eyes, you're obviously from Mediterranean descent. Franklin doesn't sound very Mediterranean."

"Why the twenty questions?"

"Because you told me years ago that you'd changed your name, but never told me why. I want to know. I'm curious. No biggie. And if we're to be an item, I don't think we should have any secrets from each other."

"Fine. My original last name was Galatos."

"Cool. Is there a meaning behind it?"

"Yeah. Apparently, it means milk seller or something. So I come from a line of milkmen or something."

"And why'd you change it?"

"Leah, really, it's not a big deal."

"Then why not share?"

Dillon sat back against the couch. She peeled at the label on her beer bottle.

"I grew up in an orphanage, if you must know the truth."

"Oh, Dillon." Leah sat closer and tried to pull Dillon to her. Dillon resisted.

"It's not a big deal. And it was a long time ago."

"Not that long ago. You're not that old."

"Old enough that enough time has passed that it doesn't matter. I survived and made something of myself. It's all good."

"Thank you, Dillon. I appreciate you sharing."

"So, what about you? Any deep dark secrets you can share?"

Leah shook her head.

"Sorry. I've got nothing."

Dillon smiled.

"Well, that's okay. I like you not having anything dark in your past. I picture you in an upper middle class neighborhood. I'm sure you took ballet and tap and all those other dance classes. You were probably a cheerleader in school, right?"

Leah laughed.

"Not quite. I wasn't all that. But I didn't grow up in an orphanage, that's for sure."

Dillon set her beer on the table and pulled Leah close.

"I hope you know how special you are to me. I don't tell just anyone about my childhood."

"I know. And I appreciate it."

She kissed Leah on the top of her head. Leah shifted and looked up at Dillon. She was so handsome. Her deep eyes were filled with desire. Leah knew she was wanted and she wanted her as well. Why couldn't they just do this?

Leah knelt and kissed Dillon on her lips. Dillon kissed her back, and Leah felt her body cover in gooseflesh. She grabbed her strong shoulders and leaned back. She wanted Dillon on top of her. She needed it.

Dillon pulled away at the last minute.

"Nice try," she said.

Leah smiled.

"I need you, Dillon."

"I need you, too."

"I really think tonight should be the night. I think we should sleep together to make sure we're compatible before we make any commitment."

"A for effort. But it's not going to happen. I need to get going."

"Please don't. At least finish your beer."

"No. I need to go."

She kissed Leah gently and let herself out.

Leah sat up on the couch and sipped her drink. Damn, Dillon had her burning so hot. She was constantly on fire any time she was near her. Why had it taken her so long to realize she wanted her that bad?

And what was stopping her from letting her in emotionally? Sure, Sueann had hurt her. She cut her deeply. But Dillon wasn't Sueann. Dillon was the most upstanding person Leah had ever met. She was caring and compassionate. And clearly she was into Leah. So what was holding her back?

She drew herself a hot bath and lit some candles. She took the remainder of her drink in with her and slipped into the bath. It felt good and helped loosen all her muscles, which had been tight with desire. While she sipped her drink, her phone buzzed. It was a text from Dillon. Her heart raced as she opened it.

Thinking of you.

That was it. That was all it said, but that was all Leah needed to get hot and bothered again. She dried her hands.

In a hot bath. Thinking of you, as well.

Nice.

Yeah. It feels good. Not as good as you would, though.
LOL Nice try, kiddo. I'm going to bed now. Good night.
Night.

Leah lay there in her tub and tried to stop her heart from racing. She had it bad. And only one person could slake her need. All those other women had meant nothing to her. She felt dirty for ever having used that stupid app. But at least this way, when she and Dillon hit the sheets, she'd be able to make Dillon feel as wonderful as she knew Dillon would make her feel.

She slid her hands down to tease her nipples as she thought of just how hot Dillon was. Her response to the touch was instantaneous. She felt her clit swell and knew this would be a short session. She closed her eyes and imagined Dillon running her hands all over her body. She arched her hips, urging her lower.

Leah moved her hand down her body until it reached her slick clit. She shuddered at the contact then slid it lower and teased her lips before sliding her fingers inside. She was so wet and so ready for Dillon. Dillon. She was all she could think about. She craved her touch, but there was something more now. She loved being around her. She couldn't wait to get to work to see her. She looked forward to her dates after work with her and their private time at her house after.

The ball inside her was tightening with her need. She slipped her hand back to her clit and rubbed it nice and easy. Her last thought before she came was that she wanted to be with Dillon.

CHAPTER TWENTY

The next morning, Leah hurried and showered. She dressed for work, taking extra time to make sure she looked her best for Dillon. This was going to be a big day. Her stomach was in knots, but she knew deep down she had made the right decision. And she knew Dillon would be thrilled with it.

She didn't even take the time to make coffee. She picked a cup up on the way in. She got to the bar and only Dillon's truck was in the parking lot. No Stephanie yet. Yay. She finished her coffee and let herself in the back door.

Leah opened the office door to find Dillon hard at work on her laptop. She looked up as Leah walked in.

"Well, good morning," Dillon said.

Leah kissed her passionately.

"Good morning to you."

"That was better than a cup of coffee to get my heart pumping," Dillon said.

"Mm. It was nice, wasn't it?"

"To what do I owe the pleasure of that?"

Leah heard the bells on the front door jingle and knew Stephanie had arrived. Damn. She'd hoped to do this before she got there.

"No reason." She sat in her chair.

"Are you sure? Because that's not the normal way you greet me at work."

Stephanie poked her head in.

"Hey, guys. Um, the coffeemaker isn't working. Will one of you come look at it?"

Dillon shot one more questioning look at Leah then left the office.

Leah's whole body was tingling after the kiss, but she knew she had to buckle down and get to work. There was a lot of money to count from the day before. She was focusing deeply on her task when Dillon interrupted her.

Her heart skipped a beat at the sight of her.

"Hey, kiddo. I've got to run out and buy a new coffeemaker. This one finally bit the dust. I don't want to wait until you run your errands."

"Okay. I'll see you when you get back."

"How much is in the budget for one?"

Leah did a quick search on their supplier's website.

"Come take a look. Which one do you think you want?"

Dillon leaned over her shoulder to look at the screen. She smelled so damned good. Her cologne was woodsy but subtle. Leah fought the urge to lick and suck her neck. They were supposed to be working, after all.

"That one looks good." Dillon pointed to one just under three hundred dollars. It had three burners, so they could keep three pots of coffee warm at one time.

"Okay. Use the bar credit card."

"Oh, I will. See you in a bit."

Leah pulled her to her and kissed her again.

"I could get used to this," Dillon said.

"Me, too."

Leah missed Dillon as soon as she was out the door. She had it bad for her and was glad she'd finally resolved to commit to her and only her. What more could she want? Who else could she need? Dillon was the complete package.

Dillon was back just after the bar opened. Leah was behind the bar with Stephanie, explaining to patrons that coffee would be made soon. There were a few grumbles, but most of them stayed and waited. They were retired and didn't have to be anywhere anyway.

Stephanie had served Martha her Bloody Mary and was visiting with her. Leah just had to keep the peace until Dillon showed up with the new machine. She was finally back and Leah's heart flip-flopped in her chest. She admired Dillon's bulging biceps as she carried the machine in.

"How's it going here?" Dillon said.

"Okay. But the natives are getting restless for their coffee."

"Just a few more minutes," Dillon said.

She got the machine hooked up, and soon the smell of fresh coffee wafted on the air. Stephanie went to work mixing Irish coffees and serving regular coffees, along with a variety of other cocktails.

"Well, if you don't need me anymore," Leah said. "I'll finish the books and get out of here so I can be back by lunch."

She went back into her office. She felt so alone. She liked being behind the bar with Dillon. She liked being anywhere with Dillon. Hell, she just liked Dillon. She got her books done and got her deposit ready to make. She said good-bye and set off on her errands.

She went to the bank first, then hit the butcher shop for burger and sandwich meats.

"Leah. I was hoping to see you here."

She turned to see Sueann standing there.

"Sueann. What are you doing here?"

"Honestly? Waiting for you."

"Why?"

"Look. Things didn't work out with me and Nadia. And I wanted to see if you wanted to give us another shot. I mean, it's been a while. I know this. But I thought maybe, just maybe you'd be willing to start dating again?"

"And you thought stalking me would be the way to ask?"

"I was going to call but wanted to see you in person. And I wanted to talk to you away from the bar, so this seemed like the best option."

"Well, to tell you the truth, it's a little creepy. More than a little. And you're wasting your time anyway. I'm seeing someone."

"Who?"

"None of your business."

Leah's order came up and she grabbed it and turned to leave. Sueann placed her hand on her arm.

"Are you sure about this, Leah? I might not give you another chance."

Like she was doing her a favor? The nerve!

"I'm sure. And please don't stalk me again." She left the butcher's shop and checked her watch. It was almost eleven. She needed to hurry to get to the bar.

Dillon saw Leah's car pull up out front and smiled.

"Man, you've got it bad, don't you?" Stephanie said.

"Hmm?" She looked over at her. "Why do you say that?"

"You see her car and you light up like a Christmas tree. Hey, I'm not knocking it. I think it's pretty cool. You two are so right for each other."

"Thanks."

Then Leah walked in. She looked like she was pissed at the world. Dillon's smile disappeared. Leah walked back to the kitchen then into the office. She didn't say a word to anyone.

"Why don't you go see what's up?" Stephanie said. "I can handle things for now."

"You sure?"

"Yeah. Go for it."

Dillon slowly opened the door to the office. She was afraid that Leah might send her away. She found her sitting in her chair with her head in her hands.

"You okay?" Dillon said.

"No."

"Want to talk about it?"

Leah looked up and Dillon could see unshed tears in her eyes. Dillon walked behind her and gently rubbed her shoulders.

"What happened out there?" she said.

"I saw Sueann."

Dillon's heart stopped. This couldn't be good.

"Where did you see her? What did she want?"

"She was waiting for me at the butcher's."

"Waiting for you?"

"Yep. She wanted to talk to me in person so thought waiting for me there would be a good idea."

"Sounds alarming to me."

"Exactly. It set off all kinds of alarms in my head. She's not okay."

"So, what did she want?" Dillon said.

"You're not going to believe this."

"Try me."

"She told me she and Nadia were through and she wanted to give me a chance to get back together with her."

"She said that?"

"Words to that effect."

"Wow. Just wow." Dillon's stomach was in knots. "So, what did you tell her?"

"What do you think? I told her I was dating someone. When she asked who I told her it was none of her business."

"Okay. Okay. Well, you need to take some deep breaths. She's out of your life now, kiddo. I'm in it. Life is looking up."

"Yeah. It really is, isn't it?"

"All right. I need to get out there and work. You try to calm down."

"Sounds good. Thanks, Dillon."

"My pleasure."

Dillon kissed her briefly then and went out to work her shift.

Leah looked better when she came out to relieve Dillon. Her color had returned to her face and she even smiled, which lit the whole room as far as Dillon was concerned. Dillon went into the office to do some work but was soon called out to help as a large group had come in for a late lunch and drinks.

She helped out as much as she could, but found herself spending much of her time watching Leah. She was beautiful. And Dillon was slowly losing her resolve to wait to take her to bed. She wanted her so bad.

"Earth to Dillon," Stephanie said.

"Yeah?"

"Would you mind bussing tables? We're almost out of glasses."

Dillon was happy to have something to do. Leah and Stephanie were great working in tandem to serve drinks. She bussed tables and washed dishes. The group was finally finished eating but stayed to drink. Combined with the happy hour crowd, they kept the three of them busy until the end of their shift.

Stephanie sat on the other side of the bar with her glass of wine.

"You two care to join me?"

"No," Leah said. "I think we're going to head out."

Dillon was surprised but didn't argue. She was ready to spend some time alone with Leah, frustrating though it was. She followed Leah to her house and walked inside with her.

"So, why no bar time tonight?" she said.

"I wanted you to myself. Is that okay?"

"Sure. I know how that feels."

"You stay here. I'll be right back."

Dillon sat on the couch and waited. Leah was back with champagne in a champagne bucket and two flutes.

"What's the occasion?" Dillon said.

Leah poured them each a glass and handed one to Dillon.

"To us," she said.

"To us."

They each took a sip. Dillon was pleasantly surprised. It was good champagne. Very good.

Leah set hers down and turned to face Dillon.

"There's something I need to tell you."

Dillon's heart fluttered. This could go either way, but the champagne was a good sign.

"Okay. Shoot."

Leah took a deep breath. She hesitated.

"Is it that bad?" Dillon said. "Should I just leave?"

"No. Oh no. Nothing like that. I'm just not sure how to say it."

"Then just say it."

"Okay. Here goes." She paused again. Her eyes watered slightly. "I love you, Dillon Franklin. And I'd be a fool if I didn't want to commit to a long-term relationship with you."

Dillon's heart beat so hard she thought it would thump out of her chest.

"Are you serious?"

"I'm dead serious."

"Oh, my God, Leah. You've made me the happiest woman on earth."

She set her glass down and pulled Leah to her. She kissed her gently, letting the softness of the kiss convey the tenderness of her feelings for her.

Leah looked at her with tears in her eyes.

"I'm sorry it took me so long to come to my senses."

"It's okay. You're here now. And nothing will ever come between us."

"Nothing and no one."

They kissed again, this one more intense. Dillon had to force herself to hold back. She wanted to take Leah right there on the couch. But that wasn't going to be the first time they made love. It would be in a bed and she would take care of Leah slowly and properly.

"I do like kissing you," Leah said. "I can't believe it took you so long to hit on me."

"Me neither. And I like kissing you, too."

They sat back and sipped some more champagne. When they'd finished their first glass, Leah picked up the glasses and the bucket and carried them to the bedroom. Dillon followed along, throbbing in her need. She knew what time it was and she was ready.

Leah set everything down on the nightstand and turned to Dillon.

"I don't know about you, but I feel like I could use a shower after that shift."

Dillon swallowed hard. Was that an invitation? Would she be strong enough not to take Leah in the shower? Her palms itched to touch her, to feel her convulsing around her.

"A shower sounds good," she said.

"Would you like to join me?"

"Of course."

Leah walked into the bathroom to turn on the shower and undress. Dillon stripped down where she was. She walked into the bathroom to see a sight she'd longed to see for years. Leah stood naked waiting for her.

"Oh, my God, you're beautiful," Dillon said. She simply stood staring at her. "Just beautiful."

"You're not so bad yourself," Leah said.

"Thanks, but I'm nothing compared to you."

She took in her sloping shoulders, soft, pale breasts, and pink nipples. She drooled over her waistline and how it flowed out gently to her shapely hips. She took a step toward Leah and stood inches away from her. She rested her hands on her hips and lowered her mouth to claim Leah's. Leah put her arms around Dillon's neck and tried to pull her against her.

"No," Dillon said. "Not yet."

"But this torture is killing me."

"Isn't it awesome?"

"No." Leah laughed. "Not really."

Dillon kissed her again and pressed their bodies together. White-hot chills swept through her body. The feeling was everything she had fantasized about and more. Leah was soft and smooth, and Dillon needed her so badly it hurt.

"We should get in the shower before we run out of hot water."
Leah's voice shook slightly.

Dillon looked deep into her eyes.

"Yeah, we should."

Reluctantly, she stepped back and allowed Leah to get into
the shower first. She followed her and closed the door behind her.
Leah was immediately back in her arms kissing her passionately.
Their tongues danced together as the water cascaded over them.
Leah broke the kiss and dropped to her knees. Dillon gently placed
her hands under her arms and stood her up.

"Not yet," she said. She took Leah's bath sponge and squeezed
her shower gel on it. She worked up a good lather then scrubbed
Leah all over. She washed every inch of her except between her
legs, taking extra care to gently wash her perfect breasts.

"What about the rest of me?" Leah said.

"You do that. I'm not touching you there until we're in bed
and I can have you properly."

"But I need you so bad."

"And I need you. But I want it to be perfect."

While Leah finished washing herself, Dillon took a washcloth
and washed herself. They rinsed and dried, and Dillon took Leah's
hand and led her to the bedroom.

"I can't believe this is finally happening," Dillon said.

"I can't believe I was blind for so long. You're the perfect
woman, Dillon."

"I'm far from perfect." She kissed a shoulder.

"You're tall, dark, and handsome with a killer body and a
wonderful personality. You're smart, caring..." Her breath caught
as Dillon nibbled on her neck. "And compassionate."

Dillon brought her mouth to Leah's and she kissed her again.
As they kissed, she walked her back to the bed. She eased her back
on it and climbed up with her.

"You're so amazingly gorgeous," Dillon said. "Every inch of
you is just beautiful."

Leah blushed under Dillon's open admiration. It started in her
chest and worked its way up to her cheeks.

"No need to be embarrassed," Dillon said. "It's the truth."

"Thank you. Will you please kiss me again?"

Dillon was happy to oblige. She kissed her on her mouth, her cheek, her ear, her neck. She kissed down to her shoulder again. She kissed the hollow at the base of her neck. She brought her hand up and gently massaged one of her breasts. Dillon ran a thumb over Leah's nipple and smiled when she felt it respond.

She moved her hand out of the way and replaced it with her mouth. She tenderly sucked on her nipple while she ran her tongue over it. She slid her hand down Leah's body and moaned appreciatively at how smooth her skin was. She slipped her hand between Leah's legs and found her hot and wet. She glided over her sleek, swollen clit and buried her fingers inside her tight center. She was soaked and closed around Dillon's fingers, welcoming them in. Dillon eased her fingers back out.

"No. Please. I need you."

She slid them back in, deeper this time. She twisted them as she pulled them out, then thrust them back in. She was working at a slow and steady pace until Leah started bucking off the bed.

"Faster, Dillon. Oh, dear God. I'm so close."

Dillon moved in and out faster then. Deeper and faster she thrust until Leah rose off the bed, frozen, and then collapsed back down. Dillon kept her fingers where they were until the inner convulsions had ceased.

She slowly withdrew herself from Leah and pulled her close.

"That was amazing," Leah said. She sounded sleepy. That was unfortunate for Dillon, since she was a mess, wet with need. But if Leah wanted to sleep, she would gladly hold her.

"Are you tired?" Leah said.

"No. Are you?"

"Not too tired."

"Are you sure?"

"Positive."

Leah propped herself up on an elbow and looked into Dillon's eyes. Dillon brushed an imaginary strand of hair off Leah's face.

She let her fingers trace her jawline. She was taken aback by the sheer beauty of Leah and was blown away that she was now hers and hers alone.

Leah kissed down Dillon's cheek and neck until she came to her chest. She left little kisses all over it until she got to her nipples. She took one then the other in her mouth, drawing them in as deep as she could. She released the nipples and kissed down her body until she was where her legs met.

Dillon braced herself for Leah's tongue. She felt her tongue tentatively licking her and felt her clit grow at the touch. Soon, Leah relaxed into it and was skillfully making love to Dillon. Dillon closed her eyes and focused on everything Leah was doing.

And then Leah slid her fingers inside.

"Oh, God. That feels good," Dillon said. "More. I need more."

Leah obliged, and Dillon knew she wouldn't last long. She tried to hold off, but the feelings Leah was creating were too strong. She closed her eyes tight. Then, she finally crossed over into oblivion and the lights behind her eyelids exploded with each orgasm that Leah created.

Leah moved up next to Dillon and Dillon wrapped her arms around her.

"You mind if I stay the night?" she said.

"I'd like it."

"Good."

Leah's breathing was becoming regular and Dillon knew she was almost asleep.

"I love you," she whispered in her ear.

"I love you, too."

EPILOGUE

Dillon stood nervously at the front of the crowd. It was the biggest day of her life and she was both excited and nervous. She knew she was doing the right thing. It was what she had dreamed of for years. She was just nervous because she wanted it to be perfect. Perfect for Leah. She had spent so much time planning it.

The music started, and Dillon turned to see Leah walking down the aisle. She took Dillon's breath away in her off-white chiffon wedding dress. It had a V-neck to tempt Dillon with her breasts and almost non-existent sleeves that showed off tanned, toned arms. She'd spent a lot of time getting ready for their wedding and it showed.

Dillon glowed with pride. Leah was about to become legally hers. They'd been living together for a year when Dillon popped the question. Leah had said yes, and here they were, a year later, getting married in front of a large group of family and friends.

Leah's father handed Leah to Dillon with a wink and a nod. Dillon took her hand and turned and faced the altar. The rest of the day passed in a blur for her. There was the ceremony, drinking and dancing after, and a good time was had by all. The only two things that stuck out in Dillon's mind were the look in Leah's eyes when she'd said "I do" and the feel of her lips when they'd kissed. Even after two years, Dillon felt a jolt of electricity shoot through her every time their lips met.

The reception was still going in full swing when Dillon and Leah said their good-byes and slipped into their changing rooms to put on their traveling clothes. Dillon wore a pair of gray slacks and a black long-sleeved shirt. She came out of her room to find Leah in a blue dress that really brought out her eyes. She moved toward her and took her in her arms. She kissed her lightly, but then her passion flared and she ran her tongue over Leah's lips. Leah backed away.

"There'll be plenty of time for that on our honeymoon," she said.

"But I need more now."

"Patience, my love."

Her love. Dillon loved to hear that. Leah loved her and now they were legally wed. No one could take Leah away from her. Ever. She smiled, thinking again of the future she and Leah would share together.

"Come on." Leah pointed to her watch. "We need to get going."

They left the reception hall and got into the waiting limousine. There was a bucket of champagne chilling in the back section. Dillon poured them each a glass.

"To us," she said.

"Forever," Leah said.

They sipped champagne on their way to the airport. They got there with plenty of time to spare. Dillon had bought them first class tickets to San Juan, Puerto Rico, where their cruise of the Southern Caribbean would begin.

"I'm so excited about our cruise," Leah said. "I've always wanted to go on one. I can't believe you found the perfect one. I can't wait to see all the exciting places. I especially can't wait to see Barbados."

"Anything for you, my wife," Dillon said.

They drank more champagne during the flight and Leah finally fell asleep. Dillon couldn't, though. It was too big of a day. She didn't want to miss a minute of it.

"Hey, kiddo," she said when they'd landed. "Come on. It's time to wake up."

"I'm sorry I fell asleep," Leah said.

"No biggie. It was a long flight."

Dillon had arranged for another limousine to take them to the Pan American Pier, from which their ship would depart. The cruise ship was huge. They had a honeymoon suite with a balcony. There was more champagne waiting for them in their suite. They opted to let it chill and went up on deck to wave good-bye with the rest of the ship goers as they pulled out of port.

The ship was filled with other lesbians, mostly couples, and it was a comfortable place for them. Dillon held Leah's hand and got a thrill every time she introduced her as her wife.

Dinner was served in the formal dining room. They were seated with three other lesbian couples. Two of them had been together for over fifteen years. One couple was celebrating five years together. They were all excited to have the newlyweds at their table.

One couple invited Dillon and Leah to go dancing with them after dinner, but Dillon declined, feigning tiredness. The truth was she'd been staring at Leah in her evening dress for too long and had to have her.

She escorted Leah back to their suite. As soon as their door was closed, she took Leah in her arms. She pressed her back against the door and kissed her with all the passion she'd kept pent up all day. Her tongue demanded entry, and Leah parted her lips to let her in. Leah tasted of the wine they'd had with dinner and that, combined with the warmth of her mouth, left Dillon dizzy with need.

When they came up for air, Leah spoke softly.

"So, did you want some champagne?" She motioned to the bucket on the table.

Dillon took a deep breath to calm her raging hormones.

"Sure."

They took the champagne to the balcony and sat in the chairs there. They watched the land getting smaller and smaller.

"So, how do you like being married, Mrs. Franklin?" Dillon said.

"So far, so good." Leah smiled.

"Here's to may years of happiness." Dillon lifted her glass.

"To happiness forever."

They sipped the champagne as they held hands. Dillon's hormones were in overdrive, but clearly Leah wanted to take it slow. She only hoped Leah wasn't too tired, because Dillon needed her. And it was their wedding night, after all.

"Are you tired, kiddo?"

"Not at all. I got a good nap on the plane. I'm just nice and relaxed."

"Excellent." Dillon looked over at her and hoped her desire was visible in her eyes.

"Don't you worry, oh wife of mine. I have plenty of energy for you."

"Good answer."

They finished their bottle of champagne, and Dillon could tell from the flush on Leah's cheeks that she was buzzed. But her eyes weren't glazed so she knew she wasn't drunk. Not too drunk to enjoy everything that Dillon had planned, anyway.

Dillon stood and took Leah's hand. She brought her to a standing position and draped an arm over her shoulders. She led her back into the cabin where she kissed her tenderly.

"You looked so beautiful at dinner. I couldn't wait to get you back here to have my way with you."

"Is that right?" Leah said.

"It is indeed." She kissed Leah again, this time lingering on her lips. "You taste like champagne."

"Imagine that. It seems that all we've done today is drink."

"We're celebrating."

"Yes, we are."

"I'm so proud to have you as my wife," Dillon said.

"I'm proud, too. I only wish I hadn't wasted all those years not seeing you when you were right in front of my face."

"Sh. You found me when you were supposed to. And now you've committed yourself to me for life. What more could I want?" She kissed her again and deftly unzipped her evening gown. Leah stood there in her in her black satin slip looking even sexier than she had in the gown. Dillon's palms itched to touch her, to take her to places only she could take her. But she didn't want to rush things. It was their wedding night and she wanted to take things slow.

"Damn, you're beautiful."

"And you're handsome. Even more so when you're turned on. Your eyes get darker and I know what's on your mind."

"You do, huh?" She smiled.

"Oh, yeah I do."

"And what might that be?" she asked before she nibbled Leah's neck.

"You want to take me and make me yours."

"I made you mine this afternoon. At the wedding."

"You know what I mean," Leah said.

"Yes, I do."

She nipped at Leah's ear and was rewarded with a sharp intake of breath. Dillon ran her hands over the slip until she brought them to rest on Leah's breasts. She caressed them through the flimsy garment until she felt Leah's nipples poke into her palms. She couldn't wait any more.

Dillon took the slip off over Leah's head and Leah stood naked before her. She pulled her against her and kissed her hard. Leah's mouth opened and their tongues danced together in practiced measure.

Dillon was on fire when she stepped back. She looked at Leah with her swollen lips and flushed body and knew she was as ready as Dillon was. Dillon slipped off her dinner jacket and moved to unbutton her shirt.

"Oh no, you don't," Leah said. "That's my job."

Leah slowly and deliberately unbuttoned every one of Dillon's buttons. She slid Dillon's shirt off her and bent to lick her nipples through her undershirt. They were responsive and soon taut. She unbuckled her belt and unzipped her pants and allowed them to fall to the floor.

Dillon stood in her boxers and undershirt.

"Are you going to finish this? Or should I?" Dillon said.

Leah ran her hands over Dillon's rock hard thighs.

"I love your body," she said.

"And I want yours. Now."

She took off her undershirt and stepped out of her boxers. She pulled Leah to her again. She moaned at the feel of Leah's flesh pressed to her own. She kissed her again and walked her back to the bed.

They lay together, with Dillon on top and kissed for what seemed an eternity. The kiss left Dillon lightheaded with desire. She moved down Leah's body until she could take her nipples in her mouth. She took one in and tweaked the other with her finger and thumb. Leah moaned her appreciation.

While she suckled her, Dillon slid a hand slowly down Leah's body until she found her wet center. She slipped one, two, three fingers inside her, and Leah arched off the bed to take them all. She moved her hips and encouraged Dillon deeper and faster. Dillon continued without missing a beat while she kissed down Leah's body and took her hard clit in her mouth. Leah pressed her face into her as she rode her, and Dillon sucked and licked until she felt Leah's insides clamp down on her fingers just as Leah screamed Dillon's name.

Dillon moved up Leah's body, dropping little kisses as she went. She finally kissed Leah on the mouth, hoping to convey her need in the kiss. She needn't have worried. As soon as the kiss was over, Leah was kissing down her body to where her legs met. Dillon spread them wider to give her more room, but Leah just placed her knees over her shoulders. She bent her head and Dillon felt her now talented tongue working its magic on her.

Dillon tangled her hand in Leah's hair as Leah brought her close to the edge before backing off. She did this several times.

Dillon was at wit's end. She needed the release that only Leah could give her.

"Please," she said through gritted teeth. "Please get me off."

Leah relinquished finally and quit teasing her. Dillon braced herself for what she knew was coming and finally rode wave after wave of orgasms as Leah catapulted her into orbit.

Leah climbed up into Dillon's arms.

"That was wonderful. At least when you finally decided to play nice," Dillon said.

Leah just smiled at her.

"I couldn't help it. I wanted to make it last."

"You were driving me crazy."

"I'd say I'm sorry…"

"Yeah. I know. You're not."

Dillon kissed Leah on the top of her head.

"You ready to get some sleep?" she said.

"I am."

"Good night, Mrs. Franklin," Dillon said.

"Good night, Mrs. Franklin."

About the Author

MJ Williamz was raised on California's central coast, which she left at age seventeen to pursue an education. She graduated from Chico State and it was in Chico that she rediscovered her love of writing. It wasn't until she moved to Portland, however, that her writing really took off, with the publication of her first short story in 2003.

MJ is the author of thirteen books, including three Goldie Award winners. She has also had over thirty short stories published, most of them erotica with a few romances and a few horrors thrown in for good measure. She lives in Houston with her wife, fellow author Laydin Michaels, and fur babies. You can reach her at mjwilliamz@aol.com

Books Available from Bold Strokes Books

Change in Time by Robyn Nyx. Working in the past is hell on your future. The Extractor series: Book Two (978-1-62639-880-1)

Love After Hours by Radclyffe. When Gina Antonelli agrees to renovate Carrie Longmire's new house, she doesn't welcome Carrie's overtures at friendship or her own unexpected attraction. A Rivers Community Novel. (978-1-63555-090-0)

Nantucket Rose by CF Frizzell. Maggie Jordan can't wait to convert an historic Nantucket home into a B&B, but doesn't expect to fall for mariner Ellis Chilton, who has more claim to the house than Maggie realizes. (978-1-63555-056-6)

Picture Perfect by Lisa Moreau. Falling in love wasn't supposed to be part of the stakes for Olive and Gabby, rival photographers in the competition of a lifetime. (978-1-62639-975-4)

Set the Stage by Karis Walsh. Actress Emilie Danvers takes the stage again in Ashland, Oregon, little realizing that landscaper Arden Philips is about to offer her a very personal romantic lead role. (978-1-63555-087-0)

Strike a Match by Fiona Riley. When their attempts at matchmaking fizzle out, firefighter Sasha and reluctant millionairess Abby find themselves turning to each other to strike a perfect match. (978-1-62639-999-0)

The Price of Cash by Ashley Bartlett. Cash Braddock is doing her best to keep her business afloat, stay out of jail, and avoid Detective Kallen. It's not working. (978-1-62639-708-8)

Under Her Wing by Ronica Black. At Angel's Wings Rescue, dogs are usually the ones saved, but when quiet Kassandra Haden meets outspoken owner Jayden Beaumont, the two stubborn women just might end up saving each other. (978-1-63555-077-1)

Underwater Vibes by Mickey Brent. When Hélène, a translator in Brussels, Belgium, meets Sylvie, a young Greek photographer and swim coach, unsettling feelings hijack Hélène's mind and body—even her poems. (978-1-63555-002-3)

A More Perfect Union by Carsen Taite. Major Zoey Granger and DC fixer Rook Daniels risk their reputations for a chance at true love while dealing with a scandal that threatens to rock the military. (978-1-62639-754-5)

Arrival by Gun Brooke. The spaceship *Pathfinder* reaches its passengers' new homeworld where danger lurks in the shadows while Pamas Seclan disembarks and finds unexpected love in young science genius Darmiya Do Voy. (978-1-62639-859-7)

Captain's Choice by VK Powell. Architect Kerstin Anthony's life is going to plan until Bennett Carlyle, the first girl she ever kissed, is assigned to her latest and most important project, a police district substation. (978-1-62639-997-6)

Falling Into Her by Erin Zak. Pam Phillips, widow at the age of forty, meets Kathryn Hawthorne, local Chicago celebrity, and it changes her life forever—in ways she hadn't even considered possible. (978-1-63555-092-4)

Hookin' Up by MJ Williamz. Will Leah get what she needs from casual hookups or will she see the love she desires right in front of her? (978-1-63555-051-1)

King of Thieves by Shea Godfrey. When art thief Casey Marinos meets bounty hunter Finnegan Starkweather, the crimes of the past just might set the stage for a payoff worth more than she ever dreamed possible. (978-1-63555-007-8)

Lucy's Chance by Jackie D. As a serial killer haunts the streets, Lucy tries to stitch up old wounds with her first love in the wake of a small town's rapid descent into chaos. (978-1-63555-027-6)

Right Here, Right Now by Georgia Beers. When Alicia Wright moves into the office next door to Lacey Chamberlain's accounting firm, Lacey is about to find out that sometimes the last person you want is exactly the person you need. (978-1-63555-154-9)

Strictly Need to Know by MB Austin. Covert operator Maji Rios will do whatever she must to complete her mission, but saving a gorgeous stranger from Russian mobsters was not in her plans. (978-1-63555-114-3)

Tailor-Made by Yolanda Wallace. Tailor Grace Henderson doesn't date clients, but when she meets gender-bending model Dakota Lane, she's tempted to throw all the rules out the window. (978-1-63555-081-8)

Time Will Tell by M. Ullrich. With the ability to time travel, Eva Caldwell will have to decide between having it all and erasing it all. (978-1-63555-088-7)

A Date to Die by Anne Laughlin. Someone is killing people close to Detective Kay Adler, who must look to her own troubled past for a suspect. There she finds more than one person seeking revenge against her. (978-1-63555-023-8)

Captured Soul by Laydin Michaels. Can Kadence Munroe save the woman she loves from a twisted killer, or will she lose her to a collector of souls? (978-1-62639-915-0)

Dawn's New Day by TJ Thomas. Can Dawn Oliver and Cam Cooper, two women who have loved and lost, open their hearts to love again? (978-1-63555-072-6)

Definite Possibility by Maggie Cummings. Sam Miller is just out for good times, but Lucy Weston makes her realize happily ever after is a definite possibility. (978-1-62639-909-9)

Eyes Like Those by Melissa Brayden. Isabel Chase and Taylor Andrews struggle between love and ambition from the writers' room on one of Hollywood's hottest TV shows. (978-1-63555-012-2)

Heart's Orders by Jaycie Morrison. Helen Tucker and Tee Owens escape hardscrabble lives to careers in the Women's Army Corps, but more than their hearts are at risk as friendship blossoms into love. (978-1-63555-073-3)

Hiding Out by Kay Bigelow. Treat Dandridge is unaware that her life is in danger from the murderer who is hunting the woman she's falling in love with, Mickey Heiden. (978-1-62639-983-9)

Omnipotence Enough by Sophia Kell Hagin. Can the tiny tool that abducted war veteran Jamie Gwynmorgan accidentally acquires help her escape an unknown enemy to reclaim her stolen life and the woman she deeply loves? (978-1-63555-037-5)

Summer's Cove by Aurora Rey. Emerson Lange moved to Provincetown to live in the moment, but when she meets Darcy Belo and her son Liam, her quest for summer romance becomes a family affair. (978-1-62639-971-6)

The Road to Wings by Julie Tizard. Lieutenant Casey Tompkins, Air Force student pilot, has to fly with the toughest instructor, Captain Kathryn "Hard Ass" Hardesty, fly a supersonic jet, and deal with a growing forbidden attraction. (978-1-62639-988-4)

Beauty and the Boss by Ali Vali. Ellis Renois is at the top of the fashion world, but she never expects her summer assistant Charlotte Hamner to tear her heart and her business apart like sharp scissors through cheap material. (978-1-62639-919-8)

Fury's Choice by Brey Willows. When gods walk amongst humans, can two women find a balance between love and faith? (978-1-62639-869-6)

Lessons in Desire by MJ Williamz. Can a summer love stand a four-month hiatus and still burn hot? (978-1-63555-019-1)

Lightning Chasers by Cass Sellars. For Sydney and Parker, being a couple was never what they had planned. Now they have to fight corruption, murder, and enemies hiding in plain sight just to hold on to each other. Lightning Series, Book Two. (978-1-62639-965-5)

Summer Fling by Jean Copeland. Still jaded from a breakup years earlier, Kate struggles to trust falling in love again when a summer fling with sexy young singer Jordan rocks her off her feet. (978-1-62639-981-5)

Take Me There by Julie Cannon. Adrienne and Sloan know it would be career suicide to mix business with pleasure, however tempting it is. But what's the harm? They're both consenting adults. Who would know? (978-1-62639-917-4)

The Girl Who Wasn't Dead by Samantha Boyette. A year ago, someone tried to kill Jenny Lewis. Tonight she's ready to find out who it was. (978-1-62639-950-1)

Unchained Memories by Dena Blake. Can a woman give herself completely when she's left a piece of herself behind? (978-1-62639-993-8)

Walking Through Shadows by Sheri Lewis Wohl. All Molly wanted to do was go backpacking...in her own century. (978-1-62639-968-6)

A Lamentation of Swans by Valerie Bronwen. Ariel Montgomery returns to Sea Oats to try to save her broken marriage but soon finds herself also fighting to save her own life and catch a murderer. (978-1-62639-828-3)

Freedom to Love by Ronica Black. What happens when the woman who spent her lifetime worrying about caring for her family, finally finds the freedom to love without borders? (978-1-63555-001-6)

House of Fate by Barbara Ann Wright. Two women must throw off the lives they've known as a guardian and an assassin and save two rival houses before their secrets tear the galaxy apart. (978-1-62639-780-4)

Planning for Love by Erin Dutton. Could true love be the one thing that wedding coordinator Faith McKenna didn't plan for? (978-1-62639-954-9)

Sidebar by Carsen Taite. Judge Camille Avery and her clerk, attorney West Fallon, agree on little except their mutual attraction, but can their relationship and their careers survive a headline-grabbing case? (978-1-62639-752-1)

Sweet Boy and Wild One by T. L. Hayes. When Rachel Cole meets soulful singer Bobby Layton at an open mic, she is immediately in thrall. What she soon discovers will rock her world in ways she never imagined. (978-1-62639-963-1)

To Be Determined by Mardi Alexander and Laurie Eichler. Charlie Dickerson escapes her life in the US to rescue Australian wildlife with Pip Atkins, but can they save each other? (978-1-62639-946-4)

True Colors by Yolanda Wallace. Blogger Robby Rawlins plans to use First Daughter Taylor Crenshaw to get ahead, but she never planned on falling in love with her in the process. (978-1-62639-927-3)

Unexpected by Jenny Frame. When Dale McGuire falls for Rebecca Harper, the mother of the son she never knew she had, will Rebecca's troubled past stop them from making the family they both truly crave? (978-1-62639-942-6)